MW00472005

Elaine

Ben Arzate

ATLATL

Atlatl Press
POB 521
Dayton, Ohio 45401
atlatlpress.com
info@atlatlpress.com

Elaine
Copyright © 2020 by Ben Arzate
Cover design copyright © 2020 by Matthew Revert
ISBN-13: 978-1-941918-58-6

This book is a work of fiction. Names, characters, business organizations, places, events, and incidents either are the product of the author's imagination or are used fictitiously. The author's use of names of actual persons (living or dead), places, and characters is incidental to the purposes of the plot, and is not intended to change the entirely fictional character of the work.

No part of this work may be reproduced, stored in a retrieval system, or transmitted by any means without the written permission of the author or publisher.

In loving memory of my Grandpa, Darrell "Buck" Jurmu
(1941 - 2019)

Also by **BEN ARZATE**

the sky is black and blue like a battered child

The Complete Idiot's Guide to Saying Goodbye

The Story of the Y

E L A I N E

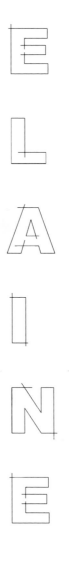

"It is clear that the world is purely parodic, in other words, that each thing seen is the parody of another, or is the same thing in a deceptive form."

— Georges Bataille, "The Solar Anus"

"It is at work everywhere, functioning smoothly at times, at other times in fits and starts. It breathes, it heats, it eats. It shits and fucks. What a mistake to have ever said the id. Everywhere it is machines—real ones, not figurative ones: machines driving other machines, machines being driven by other machines, with all the necessary couplings and connections."

— Gilles Deleuze and Felix Guattari,
Anti-Oedipus: Capitalism and Schizophrenia

"Thou shalt be for fuel to the fire; thy blood shall be in the midst of the land; thou shalt be no more remembered: for I the LORD have spoken it."

— Ezekiel 21:32

PROLOGUE

THE GRAY TABBY CAT trotted through the forest, its collar jangling and its eyes glowing in the nearly pitch-black night. It followed a dirt trail in the grass, made by feet walking over it multiple times. The cat sniffed the air. It seemed to know something unusual was this way, though it clearly didn't know what.

The cat eventually felt ash and rocks under its feet. It sniffed at the ground and sneezed. This had been a fire pit, and the fire was long out. It looked around. It saw a tent that looked like it had been hastily collapsed and torn up. Thinking it meant there was either food or people nearby, it moved toward the tent. It caught a strong whiff of blood and raw meat. It sprinted in the direction of the smell.

It soon came to the source. A young woman was sitting against a tree. Her head was down and her long hair covered her face. She was naked. Both of her breasts had been split in half. The blood stained her torso and had soaked into the ground beneath her. Her legs were open, a gaping wound between them. Her uterus and other viscera was spilled out like she had given birth to them. The cat sniffed the exposed organs and started chewing on them.

When it had its fill, it looked around some more, its mouth covered with blood. It saw another body lying on the ground nearby. The cat walked over to it. It was a young man. He was also naked but, unlike the woman, was on his back. His penis and testicles had been severed and rested on the ground beneath the wound where they once were. It looked like whoever had killed them, and it was certainly a murder, had severed their limbs at each joint. His feet had been cut off at the ankles, his lower leg at the knee, his upper at the hip. The same was true of his arm, severed at the wrists, elbows, and shoulders, and the fingers had also been cut off one by one. His face was frozen in a death mask of agony and fear.

The cat sniffed around the corpse and the bloody ground. It picked up one of the fingers in its mouth and went back the way it came. After walking in the dark forest for a while, it emerged into the dim lights coming from a row of houses. It ran between two of the houses and on to the empty road. It headed down the street until it reached the house at the end. It went around to the side of the house facing away from the rest and toward the sudden wall of pitch black the road extended into. It squatted and jumped into the open window.

Inside the living room, an old woman sat on a chair facing a fire contained in an ornate fireplace. She was reading a book. The cat sat the finger on the floor in front of her and meowed. She closed the book and set it on the arm of the chair.

"What do you have there, Prami?"

She got up and squatted down. She noticed the blood on the cat's mouth. She picked up the finger and examined it.

"You got into something, didn't you?"

She undid the cat's collar and examined it as well.

"You got some on here too. Messy cat. I'll need to get you a new one."

She walked over to the fireplace and threw the finger and the collar into the flames. She walked over to the cat and picked it up, scratching it behind its ears. The cat purred.

"Come on, sweetie," she said. "Let's get all that stuff washed off you."

ONE

CHRIS TURNED THE SIGN on the door of Snoring Records from Open to Closed.

"First part of closing up; I check the racks to make sure the customers haven't fucked the order of everything all up," he said to Primavera.

Primavera followed Chris to the shelves.

"Just make sure the artist names are in order. If it's a solo artist, go by last name. If there's a 'The' in the front, ignore that," Chris said. "Same kind of alphabetical order most places do."

"Got it," Primavera said.

Chris reached in his pocket and pulled out a set of keys and handed them to her.

"I'm going to let you take care of that, clean up, and lock up. I got to get out of here. Remember, opening time is 10 a.m. And do not lose these keys."

"Don't worry, I'll make sure everything is fine while you're gone."

"One more thing. No giving your boyfriend free records."

Primavera laughed.

"Okay. I got it. No free records for Alex."

"Thanks again for taking the job on such short notice."

"Thanks for hiring me. The money will come in handy when I start law school in the fall."

"I got to get home and finish packing. Agnes is expecting me tomorrow afternoon."

"How's she doing?"

"Eh. About as well as you'd expect when you're getting ready to bury your mom."

"Tell her I'm really sorry about what happened. It must be pretty hard."

"She'll appreciate it. You've got my number. If there's any problems, just text me."

"I will. Have a safe trip, Chris!"

Chris pulled his car into the gas station. As he was filling up the tank, his phone vibrated. It was a text from Agnes.

"Bad news. Only road to Elaine is under construction and shut down," it said.

"What do we do now?" he responded.

"There's a train station in Broken Bowl. Park there and take the train."

"Weird. Didn't know they had a train in a town that small."

"Only other way in and out. Work should be done by the time we leave. I'll pick you up at the station."

"Okay. See you tonight. Love you."

"Love you, too."

Chris looked at his car. He decided it would be safe to leave it for a few days. After all, it was a small town in Upper Michigan, not Detroit.

Chris drove past the sign that read Broken Bowl Pop. 1600. He picked up his phone and typed in "train station" on his map app. Nothing pulled up.

"Hey, how do I get to the station?" he texted to Agnes.

Agnes texted a street address back. He put it in his map app and followed it. It brought him to a small wooden building on the outskirts on the other side of town. The sign on the front read Lake Superior Passenger Railway. He parked in the small gravel lot in front. He got his backpack and suitcase out of the trunk and headed inside. The only person in the station was the overweight woman who stood behind the ticket booth reading a newspaper.

"Excuse me," he said to her.

The woman looked up from the newspaper and smiled at him.

"Hi there. How can I help you?"

"I need a ticket to Elaine. The train goes there, doesn't it?"

"It does. You're just on time. The last one comes in just ten minutes. That'll be fifteen dollars."

Chris took out his wallet and paid her. She handed him the ticket. He put it in his pocket with his wallet.

"Do I need to check my suitcase?" Chris said.

"Oh, no, don't worry about that. It's small enough to carry on. Feel free to take an ID tag though."

Chris took one of the tags from the counter. He wrote his name and address on it and tied it to the handle of the suitcase.

"Right through that way. Enjoy your trip!" The woman pointed to the door on the other side of the station.

Chris picked up his suitcase and walked through the door. Outside, the platform was bare except for a wooden bench. Beyond the two sets of train tracks, there was nothing but forest. It reminded him of something from an old movie. Before he had a chance to take a seat on the bench, he heard the train coming up the tracks. He started humming "Folsom Prison Blues" by Johnny Cash to himself. A relatively modern looking train pulled up.

I was almost expecting a steam locomotive, he thought.

It came to a stop and the door opened. He looked up and down the train and then boarded.

There was no one else inside the train. It was dead quiet. Chris took his ticket out. It didn't assign him a seat. He walked up the aisle into the next car. It was empty as well. He continued walking and found the next car was also empty.

I guess not many people are going to Elaine.

Chris felt the train lurch as it began to move. He took a seat by the window, setting his backpack on the seat next to him and his suitcase underneath it. The train clanked and screeched.

He pulled the Bluetooth earbuds from his backpack and draped them around his neck and into his ears. On his phone, he brought up the music player app and hit shuffle. "Walking Far From Home" by Iron and Wine started playing.

That's appropriate, he thought.

He stared out the window as the train picked up speed. "A Single Wish" by This Mortal Coil began to play in his earbuds as he fell asleep.

TWO

THREE

CHRIS WOKE UP TO someone gently shaking him. He looked over and saw it was a woman who looked like she worked for the train line. He pulled out his earbuds, cutting off "Someday Never Comes" by Creedence Clearwater Revival playing in them.

"I'm so sorry to wake you up, sir," she said, "but I really need to get your ticket."

She was a young, blond woman wearing a white shirt, a blue tie, a pencil skirt, and a vest. Her name tag said "Elaine."

"Yeah, let me just get it," Chris said.

He reached into his pocket and heard her snicker. He realized he was still hard from his dream and there was a noticeable bulge in his pants. He blushed, quickly fishing out the ticket from his pocket and handing it over to her.

"So, uh, Elaine," he said, "same name as the town I'm going to."

"That's right, I'm actually from there." She took the ticket and grinned.

"I'm Chris. So, uh, how long's the ride there? I'm meeting someone."

"Oh, just a little under an hour," she said. "We should arrive just before sundown."

"Where does the train go next?"

"That's our last stop. Then we turn around. I'm visiting my parents while I'm there."

"Oh, hey, I'm visiting family there, too. Maybe we'll see each other around."

"Probably. It's not a big town. I need to get back to work. Just head to the café car if you need anything. The bathrooms are on either side of each car if you need to use them."

Her eyes darted down to the bulge still in the crotch of his pants and she walked away giggling. Chris slumped in his seat. He put his earbuds back in. "Electricity" by Captain Beefheart and His Magic Band was playing.

Goddammit, he thought. *That was fucking humiliating. And what the hell was that dream? Am I some kind of pervert?*

He took his phone out of his pocket. He texted Agnes.

"Hey, I'm on the train. Should be there in about an hour. You going to be able to meet me at the station then?"

He texted Primavera.

"Everything okay at the store?"

He tried bringing up Facebook. He watched the loading circle spin for about a minute before he closed it. He looked at the signal bars on his phone. There was one that randomly appeared and disappeared.

Of course there's no signal out here, he thought.

He looked at the available Wi-Fi networks. It showed "none available."

And of course this train has no internet.

Chris sat listening to "With Whom to Dance" by the Magnetic Fields, watching the woods go by out the window.

May as well grab a pop, he thought. *Which way is the café car?*

He stood up and walked in the direction Elaine had gone.

Chris walked into the café car. It was just as empty as the rest of the train. The counter had a sign that read, "Be Right Back." Next to it was a set of vending machines. He put two quarters in one of them and selected the option for a diet cola. Nothing came out of the machine. He pressed the button again. Still nothing. He kicked the machine.

Goddammit, that was the only change I had, he thought. *I'll just wait for the cashier to come back and see if they can help out.*

He took a seat at one of the tables. He queued the album *Sung Tongs* by Animal Collective on his phone. After ten minutes, no one had come to the counter.

Fuck it, he thought. *He got up and headed back to his seat.*

He checked his phone as he walked back. Both texts he'd sent were still in "sending" status.

I guess I'll just call Agnes when I get there, he thought.

When he got back to his seat, both his backpack and his suitcase had been opened and rummaged through.

"What the fuck!" Chris said.

He pulled his earbuds out of his ears. He went through his bags, closing them back up when he was finished.

Doesn't look like anything was taken, he thought. *Was it that Elaine girl?*

He looked around. He was still the only one in the car.

Fuck this shit, he thought. *I'm just going to sit here and complain at the station.*

He sat down and put one of his earbuds back in, continuing to listen to the Animal Collective album. He kept his hands on his suitcase and his backpack on his lap as the train rolled on.

FOUR

IT WAS TWILIGHT OUTSIDE when the train started slowing down. The station in Elaine was just as small and old as the one in Broken Bowl.

Fucking finally, Chris thought.

The train stopped. Chris grabbed his suitcase, threw his backpack over his shoulder, and walked out the nearest door as soon as it opened. On the platform, he turned around and watched the doors, waiting to see if anyone else would come out. He felt his phone vibrate in his pocket. It was a text from Primavera.

"Hey, everything went okay today. Not very busy. You make it up okay?"

He texted back, "Just got to Elaine. Had to take a train because the road was out."

He watched the text's status sit on "sending" again. The phone still only had one bar at best.

Of course, he thought.

He checked the text he'd sent to Agnes. It still showed as stuck in "sending."

Weird, why didn't the one for her go through? he thought. *I'll call her. Hopefully that will work.*

He selected the call option on Agnes's number. The call went through, but a message indicating it went straight to voicemail was the only response. He hung up.

Is her phone off? What the hell? She knew I was coming.

He sighed and took another look around. No one else had

exited the train. He went inside the station. It looked almost exactly the same as the one in Broken Bowl and was just as empty. Even the woman at the ticket counter looked like a thinner version of the one who sold him his ticket. She stood with her arms folded on the counter and her head down, looking like she was asleep on her feet.

Chris approached her.

"Excuse me," he said.

Her head shot up.

"What!" she started. "Oh! I'm so sorry, sir! We don't get much business and I just nodded off!"

"Don't worry, I run a store and I've done the same thing."

"How can I help you? I'm afraid if you need a train, there's no more today."

"I know, I just arrived on the last one. I've got a complaint."

"Oh no! Well, I can certainly take that for you. What's wrong?"

"I left my bags at my seat for a little bit. When I came back, someone had opened and gone through them. I don't think there were any other passengers, so I think it was someone on the staff."

"That's awful! Did they steal anything?"

"I don't think so."

"I know that must be very upsetting. I do have to let you know that the train company isn't liable for anything stolen, lost, or damaged. You may want to check your bags next time to make sure they're secure."

"But the lady in Broken Bowl said . . ."

Chris sighed.

"Never mind," he said. "Can you just have them look into this girl named Elaine who took my ticket? I think she might have done it."

"Oh, what a coincidence! My name is Elaine, too."

"Huh."

"I'll send a notice to the manager to have him speak with her. Is there anything else I can help with?"

"Does this station have Wi-Fi?"

"I'm afraid it doesn't, sir."

"Can you give me a phone book or something? My girlfriend was supposed to pick me up, and I think her phone is dead because I can't reach her. I need to find her dad's number or something."

"Oh my. Yes, there's a phone book by that pay phone over

there."

She pointed to a pay phone hanging on the wall. Chris was surprised it was there. He hadn't seen one in a long time. It looked like it was in good condition, too. The phone book dangling on a chain under it looked worn but mostly well preserved. It was like they were used and replaced as commonly as they were back in 1995. Now that he thought about it, the whole station looked like it was frozen in 1995.

He walked over to the phone and started going through the phone book.

Let's see, he thought, *J for Jespersen. Looks like there's only one here. Karl and Susanna. That's Agnes's parents, all right.*

He dialed the number on his phone. It rang twice before a man picked up.

"Yeah, hello?" he said.

"Hi, is this Karl Jespersen?"

"That's who you're speaking to."

"It's Chris here. You know, Agnes's boyfriend?"

"Oh, yeah! How are you doing, young man?"

"Well, I'm here in town at the train station. Agnes was supposed to come get me, but she's not here and she's not answering her phone."

"Uh oh. She went to see one of her old friends last I saw of her. Don't got another ride?"

"Nope. I had to leave my car back in Broken Bowl and take the train."

"That's right, the road being out and all. Don't you worry! Just wait in front of the station and I'll come get you."

"Thanks, man."

"I'll give Agnes a good talking to when she gets home."

Chris stood in the gravel lot of the train station. He took out his phone and pulled up Google. He typed "Lake Superior Passenger Railway." He watched the loading bar crawl slowly across the top of the screen until it stopped in the middle. He waited for several minutes until he clicked the screen off and shook his head. His phone vibrated. He received another text from Primavera.

"Glad you got there. A train? They have that up there?"

He texted back, "I know. We don't even have a train that goes through Monk City. I was the only passenger. Signal sucks up here, by the way."

He checked the texts he sent to Agnes. They were still showing as "sending."

A black pickup truck pulled into the gravel lot and parked near the front of the station. An older man with white hair, heavy bags around his eyes, and his chin and cheeks covered in stubble leaned out.

"Hey, are you Chris?" he said.

"That's me. Are you Agnes's dad?"

"Yup. Hop on in! Just throw that suitcase in the back."

Chris set the suitcase in the corner of the bed of the truck. He climbed in the passenger side, setting his backpack on the floor in front of him. The man pulled the truck out of the gravel lot.

"So, do you go by Karl?" Chris said.

"Yup, and you just go by Chris?"

"Yeah. Sorry we couldn't meet under better circumstances. I'm really sorry about your wife."

"Well, thank you, young man. It's been tough, but having Agnes back really helped."

"You said that she was at a friend's place?"

"She left this morning. Said she was going to meet her old friend. A girl named Elaine who she knew back in high school."

"Really? There are a lot of women here named Elaine, huh?"

"What do you mean?"

"Well, the woman at the counter in the station was named that. The one who took my ticket on the train here was too."

"Well, that's the damnedest thing. Anyway, she left to see her this morning and I haven't heard from her since. She didn't tell me you'd be arriving today. Must've slipped her mind."

"I hope nothing's wrong. I can't reach her phone at all."

"Aw, it probably died because she forgot to plug it in. She's been making little mistakes like that all the time. Her mother dying has her head in a whirl."

"That's probably it."

"Besides, I'm sure you seen that the signal is for shit here. Never bothered to get a cell phone myself. Hell, I still got a rotary. If it ain't broke, why replace it?"

Chris looked out the window. There was nothing beside the road except woods illuminated by the truck's headlights, occasionally punctuated by the lights of a small house.

"My record player, too," Karl said. "I've had that thing since 1973. Works as well as the day I bought it. Only ever had to replace the needle once. How are things going at your store, by the way?"

"Pretty good. I hired someone to look after the place while I'm up here."

"I'm surprised you still sell actual records and not just CDs. I thought everyone was getting music off the internet now."

"Well, a lot of people are, but that actually helped vinyl. Records usually sound better than what you get off streaming, especially if you've got a good setup. Plus, a lot of records will give you a free download for the music too."

"'Streaming, downloading.' I guess that's all internet stuff. Ain't had a computer since Agnes left and took hers, so I don't know at all about that. Probably should. Seems like everything is on there now."

"Pretty much. Did you like those Etta James records Agnes brought up? She said you were a big fan."

"Oh, yeah. They're great! I was damn glad she brought them. Elaine had a record store, but it closed back in '91. Got to drive over an hour to Pletschke if you want to shop for music now."

"Maybe I could open a franchise in Elaine or something if business picks up enough."

"Well, I'd sure be happy to run it for you if you do that. Ain't much going on in town since the paper factory closed. Ope. Our house is just up here."

Karl parked the truck in the driveway.

"That's a pretty nice house," Chris said.

"Well, thank you, young man. We moved in not long after Agnes was born. It's the perfect location. Right between the beach on Lake Superior and town. Could walk to either if you want to, but my knees are too bad to do too much walking now."

As Chris stepped out of the truck, his phone vibrated. It was a text from Agnes.

"Really sorry. Things came up at Elaine's place. Staying night here. Be back tomorrow morning."

Chris texted back. "Everything okay?"

He watched the status sit on "sending" again.

"Everything all right?" Karl said.

"I just got a text from Agnes. She said she's staying the night at her friend's place. I'm kind of worried."

"Aw, I'm sure it's okay. She probably just had trouble being in the house with Sue gone. First night I had to spend without her, I took an air mattress down to the beach to sleep. I just couldn't sleep in our bed without her."

"That might be it."

"Look at it this way, I made pasties for supper and that means more for us. And I guarantee the recipe my wife left me is the best pasty in the entire UP!"

Chris sat at the table waiting for Karl to bring the pasties. He looked around.

This reminds me a lot of my grandma's house, he thought. *It's like every old person in the Midwest has the same interior decorator.*

"Miller Lite all right for you to drink?" Karl called from the kitchen.

"Yeah, that sounds good."

A moment later, Karl came from the kitchen. He carried a tray with several pasties and two cans of Miller Lite. He set one can in front of Chris and the tray in the middle of the table. He sat down.

"Dig in!" Karl said. "Have as many as you can want. Careful, they're still kind of hot."

The smell hit Chris as he took one and started cutting off a piece. He hadn't realized how hungry he was. Before he knew it, he'd devoured it and was reaching for another.

"Wow, these are delicious," he said.

"I knew you'd love them. I can freeze some for you to take home. Did that for Agnes last time she visited."

"Too bad she kept them to herself."

Karl laughed. "Even the most generous Yooper turns greedy when it comes to pasties."

"You sure I can't help with the dishes?" Chris said.

Karl was gathering up the plates on the empty tray. Chris was surprised the two of them had managed to finish all of them.

"You're a guest here. Besides, I've got to learn to do them

myself with Sue gone. You just make yourself at home. Watch some TV in the living room or something and relax. I'll show you the guest room when I'm done."

Well, there's not much else to do, Chris thought.

He walked into the living room and sat in a recliner. He picked up the remote from the coffee table and turned on the TV. A blond woman was giving a weather report from a local station. He could see that some of the report on the green screen was visible over her blouse. He laughed.

She must be new. I would have thought someone there would tell her not to wear green, he thought.

The report was predicting clouds, wind, and occasional rain for the entire Porcupine Mountains area for the rest of the week. The weather woman cheerfully told the audience to make sure to bring their umbrellas and raincoats on their way to work tomorrow because there would be heavy rain by the evening commute.

The funeral's going to be really dreary, Chris thought.

Karl came into the living room and sat in the chair next to Chris.

"I remember her," Karl said. "She was another one of Agnes's friends back in high school. I didn't think she was the type to stay up here and be a weather girl. She always wanted to be a marine biologist."

"Things don't always work out. I wanted to be a rock star when I was a kid."

"You play guitar?"

"Yeah. I played in a couple bands that never went anywhere. I still play covers at the occasional open mic."

"Well, that's good. Are there even rock stars anymore? It seems that rap crap is all I hear on the radio."

Chris rolled his eyes.

"That is the most popular kind of music right now, yes."

"I don't get that stuff. It's nothing but jungle chanting."

Oh Christ, Chris thought.

On the TV, the weather woman finished her report.

"Back to you, Greg and Elaine!" she said in her chipper voice.

"Thank you, Elaine!" the anchor, Greg, said. "Coming up when we return, we'll have Sean with sports and an update on the missing teenage couple from Ironhorse. We'll hear from a truck driver who claims to have given them a ride while they were hitchhiking."

Chris stared at the TV as the news jingle played and the screen faded to a commercial.

"How many women in this town are named Elaine?" Chris said.

"Hmm?"

"Like, every woman up here I've seen, besides Agnes, is named Elaine."

"Guess I just didn't notice."

"But I told you . . ."

Chris sighed.

"Never mind. Hey, uh, can you show me to that guest room? I've had a long day and I want to go to bed soon."

"Course! Go grab your stuff. The room's upstairs."

Chris carried his backpack and suitcase up the stairs, following Karl, who seemed to struggle with each step.

"I got some advice for you," Karl said. "Don't get old. Your knees go to shit and this happens."

Chris laughed politely.

"You're doing better than my dad. He messed up his leg and needs a cane to get anywhere now."

"Oh, no. How'd he do that?"

"Falling down some stairs, actually."

"Well, thanks for the comforting thought!"

They reached the top of the stairs. Karl led Chris to a door at the end of the hall. Inside was a bedroom with little more than a bed, a nightstand, and a painting of a boat on a lake hanging on the wall.

"It ain't much, but we don't get many guests," Karl said.

"Nah. It's pretty nice. A lot cleaner than my place."

"You need Agnes to whip you into shape. Sue never tolerated messes and she inherited that."

Chris set his suitcase and backpack on the floor.

"Hey, I know it's early, but I'm dead tired. I'm going to go to bed."

"All right then. The bathroom's just across the hall if you need it. Let me know if you need anything else."

"Okay. Thanks a lot."

"Oh, it's no problem! Thank you for coming up for Sue's funeral."

Karl headed back down the hall. Chris watched as he slowly began to descend the stairs.

He closed the door. He took his pajamas from his suitcase and changed. He took his phone charger from his backpack. He plugged his phone into the outlet next to the nightstand and made sure the alarm was set. He selected his "Sleep" playlist on his music player app and climbed into bed. "Goodnight Georgie" by Clinic played as he fell asleep.

FIVE

***CHRIS IS BACK ON** the train. He looks around. It's pitch black outside. He walks to a window. He presses his face against it. He can't see anything. It's like the outside of the window is painted black. He walks to the nearest door to the outside. He tries to force it open. It won't budge. He walks into the next car. It looks the same as the previous one. He walks to the next one. Then the next one. Then the next one. He starts running. The train cars seem to endlessly repeat. He opens the door to one and sees someone standing in the middle. She's wearing the same uniform as Elaine from the train except her hair is black. He calls out to her. He approaches her. She turns around. It's his sister, Amy. She's clutching something in her hand. She says she's sorry, but she's the one who went through his luggage. He asks her why she did that. She opens her hand. She reveals a crumpled pair of panties. She says she knows he stole these from her drawer. Chris denies it. She slaps him. She calls him a liar. She calls him a pervert. He tries to defend himself. He says he hasn't been in her room in years. She stuffs the panties in his mouth. She pushes him. He falls on his back. She steps on his groin. His cock is hard in his jeans. She steps down hard. She calls him pathetic. He tries to pull her panties out of his mouth. She kicks his hand. She tells him she'll kick his head in if he takes them out. He starts crying through his gag. She calls him a crybaby. She says he was always a crybaby. She grinds her foot into his groin. She laughs. He tries to squirm away. She kicks his torso. She tells him to stay still. She grinds and stomps on his cock through his jeans. He groans into his gag with each blow. His body tenses up. He realizes he's going to ejaculate. She asks if he's going to* *cum. She laughs. She tells him he's disgusting. She stomps on his groin repeatedly. He quietly cries though the panties in his mouth as he feels himself cum.*

SIX

CHRIS WOKE UP TO the rooster sound that was set as the alarm on his phone. He reached over and shut the alarm off. He quickly realized his pajama pants felt wet.

Oh, fuck me, you've got to be kidding, he thought.

He felt the crotch of his pants and could feel the sticky spot.

Goddammit. Dreaming about that shit again, and it was a fucking wet dream, too. I must really be a pervert.

Chris got out of bed and looked in the hall. Seeing that no one was there, he went into the bathroom. He locked the door. He washed the crotch of his pajama pants in the sink and hung them up on the rack. He got in the shower.

Damn, what's wrong with me? he thought as he washed himself. *Do I really want to fuck my sister? Is that why we haven't talked in so long? Is that why we could never get along? God, I hope not. I should call her up when I get home.*

He got out of the shower and looked at his pajama pants.

That'll have to do until I can get it washed.

He put the pajamas back on and went back into the bedroom. He looked at his phone. He noticed it was only at two percent power despite being plugged into the wall. It wasn't charging. He tried unplugging it and plugging it back in, but it still wouldn't charge.

What the fuck? Is it my phone? Shit!

He got dressed and headed downstairs, his dying phone in his pocket and the charger in his hand. He looked around downstairs.

It was quiet. He couldn't see Karl anywhere.

"Karl?" he said. "Agnes?"

There was no answer.

He must still be asleep, he thought.

He found an outlet in the living room and plugged his phone in. It started charging.

Oh good, it was just the outlet.

He left his phone to charge and went out the front door. Everything seemed to have a blue tint in the early morning light. He looked around, hoping to see Agnes's car, but it was nowhere in sight. He took a deep breath and sighed. He could faintly hear the waves of Lake Superior coming from behind the house. He looked up at the sky. Clouds were starting to move in, but it was still mostly clear.

She must be on her way. I'll take a walk and she should be here by the time I get back.

He went behind the house and saw a trail leading into the woods. He started following it. He listened to the sounds of birds chirping, the rustling of brush, and the waves of the lake which got louder as he continued to walk. The trail started changing from dirt to sand as he got closer to the lake.

He emerged from the forest on to a beach. He walked in the sand, staring at the horizon where the sky met the lake. He swore he could see something on the horizon and briefly wondered if he was looking at Canada. He breathed in the air and listened to the waves, feeling peaceful.

His peaceful state was gently interrupted by a snorting sound and something pressing into his crotch. He looked down and laughed when he saw the Malamute sniffing at him. He knelt and started petting the dog's head.

"Hey there, buddy," he said to the dog. "Where'd you come from, huh?"

A woman jogged up to Chris and the dog. When he looked up at her, he was surprised and a little frightened. She was a dead ringer for Amy, but for some minor details on her face. The tight, brightly colored workout spandex she was wearing did little to assuage his feelings of confusion.

"Oh, I'm so sorry," she said. "Is my dog bothering you?"

"Oh, no! Not at all!"

He stood up. The dog trotted over to his owner. She bent over and scratched behind its ears.

"Didn't I tell you not to run off, Abe?" she said to the dog. "I did. Yes, I did."

Chris struggled to keep his eyes off her breasts in her tight top, feeling ashamed.

"So, uh, Abe like Abe Lincoln is his name?" he said.

"He's named after my grandpa Abram."

"Aw, that's sweet. My name's Chris, by the way."

He held out his hand. She shook it as she smiled at him.

"I'm Elaine, it's nice to meet you. Are you new in town?"

"Um . . . Er . . . Well, I'm actually up here visiting some family."

"I see. There's not many visitors that come here. This isn't exactly a tourist hotspot."

"It is a nice place. Tourists would probably ruin it."

Elaine laughed.

"That's true. Hey, I have to get back home. Maybe I'll see you around. It is a pretty small town."

"Yeah, maybe! See you!"

"Come on, Abe."

Elaine and the dog turned and jogged away. Chris couldn't help but stare at her backside as it moved in the tightly hugging workout pants, feeling the blood running to his penis. She turned and gave a knowing grin. He didn't know what else to do but grin back. His hard-on pressed painfully against his jeans.

After she was out of sight, Chris slapped himself on the side of his head. He turned around and headed back up the trail.

"What the fuck is wrong with you!" he mumbled to himself. "You're up here for your girlfriend's mother's funeral, and you're flirting with a girl that looks like your fucking sister! You piece of shit! You're the worst kind of man! I should bash your head into one of those fucking trees! Get your fucking brain cleaned out!"

He kept mumbling to himself as he walked up the trail until he reached the house. He went back around the front and looked around. Agnes's car still wasn't there.

Where is she? he thought. *Well, at least I didn't run into her with my mind all fucked up like this.*

He saw a newspaper by the door and picked it up. The headline announced a factory in Broken Bowl would be closing down. He walked inside the house and the smell of bacon cooking filled his nostrils. He went to the kitchen and saw Karl hunched over the stove in a robe and pajama pants. Karl looked over and saw Chris.

"Good morning!" Karl said. "I figured you'd be up early."

"Morning. Do you know if Agnes is on her way back?"

"If she is, she hasn't called or anything. She text you?"

"I'll check. By the way, is that outlet in the bedroom not working? It didn't charge my phone."

"Ah, yeah. Sorry, forgot to tell you. Sometimes it works and sometimes it don't. It's only that outlet, so I never bothered to have it looked at."

"It's no problem. I brought in your paper, by the way."

"Well, thanks! That's very kind of you."

Chris handed him the paper and went to check his phone. There were no new texts. He checked the last one he'd sent, and it said it had delivered. He also saw that his phone had only charged up to three percent.

What the hell? he thought. *Maybe my phone is fucked.*

He sighed and set his phone back down.

Chris sat at the table sipping coffee. His bacon and eggs were barely touched. His appetite wasn't nearly as strong as it had been the previous night.

"Do the outlets in the living room ever have any problems?" he said to Karl.

Karl looked over his paper.

"Not that I know of. Why?"

"Well, my phone didn't charge much, and I left it on there for a while."

"That's odd. Is the phone having problems?"

"It might. You didn't unplug it, like, on accident or anything?"

"Nope. Haven't touched it."

"I know the signal isn't great, but I'd hate to be up here with my phone fucked."

"You're free to use my phone if you need to make a call. And there's always the library if you need to use the internet. I'll take you there later if you want."

"Thanks. I wonder where Agnes is. I thought she'd be here by now."

"I'm wondering, too. Poor girl must be even more broken up

about her mother than she wanted to show."

"I'm really starting to get worried about her."

"Aw, she's a strong girl. She'll be coming through that door any time now."

"I hope so."

Chris took a few more bites of his breakfast. He set his fork down.

"I'm sorry," he said. "It's good, but I'm just not hungry."

"You ate a lot last night and you're a skinny guy. Let me have that. I'm always starving in the morning. You go on and watch TV or something until Agnes gets here."

Chris pushed his plate to Karl. Karl scraped the food on to his own as Chris stood up and went into the living room.

He checked his phone. It had charged to fifteen percent.

I guess it is working, he thought. *Maybe it just had a hiccup.*

He turned on the TV. A commercial for a car dealership in Ironhorse was just coming to an end. A station identification and a schedule of the next few programs came on. It said the next show coming up was "The Morning Sermon with Pastor Toivo."

He picked up the remote and was about to change the channel when the program started. An out of tune organ played a hymn over a title card with the name of the show in an ornate font. He chuckled at how ridiculous it looked. He set the remote down.

To his surprise, the title card faded into a simple wooden desk in front of an off-white wall. A man in a gray suit who looked like he was in his late fifties took a seat behind the desk, setting a Bible on it.

Top notch production values, Chris thought.

"Good morning, brothers and sisters in Christ," the man said. He spoke with an accent Chris couldn't place. "I am Pastor Toivo and thank you for joining me. Today's reading is from Judges 11."

The man opened his Bible and began reading. The camera remained fixed on him as he read a story about an Israeli military leader who promised to sacrifice the first thing that came out of his house if God granted him victory in battle. Chris found himself taken in by the way the man spoke. The story took a dark turn when the leader returned home and his only daughter was the first thing that came out. The girl agreed to be sacrificed willingly if her father gave her two months alone to mourn. Chris expected the story to end with the daughter running away or God intervening to change the man's mind. To his surprise, the girl returned and was sacrificed as her father promised.

They never told me that story in Sunday school, Chris thought. *That's just morbid and pointless. Where is he going with this?*

"Now as you can see, Jephthah and his daughter knew in their heart of hearts that a promise to the Lord comes above all else. Even one's own family. So many these days will place the obligations of the ephemeral material world above those of the Kingdom of the Almighty. Though it was painful for the young lady and her father, they willingly made the sacrifice."

Chris rolled his eyes and picked up the remote.

"I can't imagine the pain the young woman must have felt as she lay there on the sacrificial altar burning," Pastor Toivo said. "Writhing in agony as the flames licked at her young flesh."

Chris froze.

Wait, what?

"And how distraught Jephthah must have been! Having to strip his beautiful daughter naked and tie her to that altar. Yet, how full of the Holy Spirit he must have been! How excited he must have been to send his daughter into the waiting arms of the Lord!"

That wasn't in the story. What the hell?

The pastor on the TV was getting even more visibly excited. He waved his arms and closed his eyes as if in ecstasy.

"The blood must have run hot through his veins! What restraint it must have taken not to take his daughter's virginity before his sacrifice, knowing that the Almighty much prefers the flesh of virgins! Wh—"

Chris turned the TV off.

"Jesus Christ," he said. "What the fuck?"

"Something wrong?"

Chris started and turned around. He was relieved when he saw Karl standing there.

"Yeah!" Chris said. "There was this preacher on TV and he was talking about human sacrifice and a guy raping his daughter and shit!"

"Oh, were you watching Pastor Toivo's show?"

"Yeah, that's his name! What the hell was that? That guy's crazy!"

"He's just a little overzealous when he preaches. I used to go to his church. You should have seen him at the pulpit."

"That wasn't just 'overzealous.' He seemed like he was getting off talking about all that shit. It was fucking creepy."

"Ah, don't pay him any mind. He always sounds like a kook to people the first time they hear him. I can introduce you. He's pretty nice when he's not giving his sermons."

"No way! I want to stay far away from him!"

"Suit yourself. Agnes gotten a hold of you? She still isn't here."

Chris picked up his phone and checked it. It had charged to fifty percent, to his relief, but there were no messages from Agnes.

"Nope," Chris said. "No messages. I'm going to call her and see what's up."

He selected call and heard the phone ringing on the other end. Finally, it went to voicemail.

"Hey, call me when you get this," he said and hung up.

"She didn't answer?" Karl said.

"No. Now I'm really worried."

"Aw, I'm sure she was just in the bathroom or something and left her phone out. I'll bet she'll call back in a little bit."

"I think we should go to her friend's house and see what's going on."

"Well, I don't got much else going on today. Give me a minute to get ready and I'll drive you over."

Chris rode in the front seat of the truck as Karl drove through town. It looked like the downtown of every other small town with its lines of shops on its main street, many of which clearly hadn't been in business for years. Karl parked the truck in front of a building that housed two businesses, one of which was empty and had a faded sign that read "E&E Barber Shop" hanging over it. The other appeared to be a knickknack store called "Elaine and Maija's Gifts." In the middle was a third door with no sign above it.

"This is the building Elaine's apartment is in," Karl said.

"Well, her car's not here," Chris said.

"She might have left. Better see if she left her phone there or something."

"Good idea."

"Through that middle door and up the stairs. Elaine's apartment is through the door on the right at the top. You mind going up to check yourself? It's a long way up with no elevator and you know how I am with stairs."

"All right. I'll be right back."

Chris followed Karl's instructions. The hallway at the top of the stairs had two doors on either side. Chris knocked on the one to the right.

"Just a moment!" a voice from the other side said.

After a moment the door opened. The woman from the beach stood there in a short robe. Her wet hair was draped over her shoulders. The top of her robe was open just enough to see her cleavage.

"Well, this is unexpected," Elaine said. "Are you stalking me?"

She giggled.

Ah, shit, Chris thought.

SEVEN

CHRIS STOOD DUMBSTRUCK, trying to find something to say.

"Are you just going to gawk, or do you want to come in?" Elaine said.

"Oh, uh, yeah. Okay."

Chris walked inside past Elaine. She shut the door. The apartment was much bigger than he expected. The ceiling was high. The living room still had plenty of room even with two couches, four chairs, and the large flat screen TV. On the other end of the living room, a portrait of the Brooklyn Bridge covered the entire wall. Near the front door was the entrance to the kitchen.

"Just have a seat anywhere you'd like," Elaine said. "I'm going to get some coffee. Would you like a cup?"

"Okay, thanks."

Chris took a seat in one of the chairs as Elaine went into the kitchen. He examined the details of the Brooklyn Bridge portrait.

So, I guess just tell her the truth, he thought. *I'll look like a huge asshole, but that'll save me from being an even bigger one.*

Elaine walked into the living room, handed him a mug of hot coffee, and sat in the chair across from him. She crossed her legs and took a sip of her coffee.

"So, to what do I owe this visit?" Elaine said, smirking. "I didn't expect to see you again so soon."

"Well, I'm looking for my girlfriend, Agnes. She said she came here and now I can't get a hold of her."

"Ah. So, you're Agnes's man. She didn't tell me you were in

town. It's a shame about her mother."

"Yeah. I came up here for the funeral."

"She stayed over last night, but I don't know where she went. She was gone when I woke up this morning."

"Okay, that's really weird. She didn't leave her phone here or anything, did she?"

"I don't think she did. She seemed pretty torn up about her mom. She probably just needs some alone time."

"Even so, I'd like to at least get a call or text from her saying she's okay."

"I'm sure she'll call. You seem really tense."

"I mean, yeah. It's really not like her to just go dark on that."

"She's had a serious loss. People cope with it in different ways. Just relax."

Elaine uncrossed her legs. Under her robe, Chris could see her pussy and the trimmed tuft of pubic hair above it. She quickly crossed her legs again. Chris started when he realized what he'd seen and spilled some of the hot coffee on his thigh.

"Ouch! Fuck!" he said.

"Oh. It didn't burn you, did it?"

"No, no. I'm fine. Can I use your bathroom?"

"Sure. It's at the end of that hall to the left. Need any help?" Elaine grinned.

"No, I'll be okay, thanks. Just going to make sure it doesn't stain."

Chris got up and headed down the hall next to the living room, passing three rooms. Looking back, he could see there were two more rooms in the other direction.

Man, this a pretty big apartment. Way bigger than mine, he thought.

Chris went into the bathroom at the end of the hall. He grabbed a washcloth hanging from the hook on the wall, wet it in the sink, and started scrubbing the coffee stain on his jeans. As he started drying it with a towel his mind wandered back to the brief moment when Elaine flashed herself to him. He felt his hard-on grow.

Goddammit, no! Get your mind off that!

He ran the cold water in the sink and splashed a handful on his face. He exited the bathroom and noticed the second door from the end of the hall was open. Inside, the room was mostly empty but for some pet toys and a small dog bed in the corner with Elaine's Malamute fast asleep. The thing that stood out the most was the vault door on the opposite end.

The hell? Is she rich or something?

He went back into the living room where Elaine was still sipping from her coffee cup.

"I'd better get going," he said. "I need to figure out where Agnes is. Do you have any idea where she went?"

"Not at all," Elaine said. "I thought she was going home. Are you sure you can't stay?"

"No, no. Her dad gave me a ride and he's waiting for me downstairs."

"My door's open if you want to come back."

She smiled at him. He smiled back and hurried out the door.

Why does she want to fuck me so bad? he thought as he went down the stairs. *Is she trying to make Agnes jealous or something?*

The Butthole Surfers' rendition of "American Woman" played in his head. When he got to the bottom of the stairs, he found a piece of paper hung on the door with electrical tape.

Chris,
Had to run off real quick. Will be back ASAP. Just wait here.
—Karl.

Chris sighed and stuffed the note into his back pocket. He opened the door and saw that Karl's pickup was gone.

What the hell? he thought.

As he looked up and down the street, his phone vibrated. He quickly took it out. There was a message from Primavera.

"Hey, there's a customer who wants to special order an album, but I can't find it in any of the databases."

He texted back, "It's probably out of print. Write down the information for the album and the customer's contact email. I'll look for it when I get back."

He checked the last text he'd sent to Agnes. It said it had been sent and was delivered. He sent her another one.

"Look, I'm getting worried about you. Just text me to let me know you're fine."

He looked up and down the street again and felt his phone buzz in his hand. Agnes had texted back.

"I'm fine," it said.

"What is going on?" he responded.

He watched the screen, hoping she would respond right away again. After a minute, he realized she wasn't going to. He sighed and dropped his arms to the side. He slid his phone back in his pocket. He looked around, realizing the street was empty.

You'd swear this was a ghost town, he thought. *I'm not standing out here.*

He walked into Elaine and Maija's Gifts. He started at the noise when the door opened. Realizing it was a bell above the door, he ran his palm down his face. He started looking at the nearest rack of items. All of them were Precious Moments figurines. He picked one up, an angel holding a tablet with a Bible quote, and read it.

Psalm 137:9
Blessed shall he be who takes and dashes your little ones against the rock.

He was about to put it back on the shelf, then did a double take.

"Wait, what!" he said.

"Can I help you?" a voice said from behind him.

Chris started and dropped the figurine. It fell to the floor and shattered.

"Sorry! I'll pay for that!" he said, bending down to scoop up the pieces of ceramic.

He stood up and turned around, holding the pieces in the palm of his hand. He saw an old woman with a stern look on her face standing there. She held out her hand.

"Please give me that," she said.

He slid the pieces into her hand. He watched as she went behind the counter at the front of the store, throwing them in what he assumed to be a trash can.

"Are you going to pay now, or do you want to do some shopping first?" she said.

"Um . . . I'll just pay for it and go," Chris said, approaching the counter.

"I'm fine with you shopping here. It was an accident. I just need you to pay for it."

"Well, I'm just waiting for a friend anyway."

Chris pulled his wallet out.

"How much was it," he said.

"A hundred and twenty-five dollars."

"What? Those things cost that much? Seriously?"

"They're limited editions."

"You've got to be . . . Okay, okay. Do you take cards?"

"For that I can."

He handed her his credit card. She reached under the counter and brought out a manual card imprinter.

"Wow," Chris said. "I haven't seen one of those in a while."

"I believe if it works, there's no need to replace it."

The woman ran the slide over the card. She handed it back to Chris along with the sheet.

"Sign here, please," she said.

"You know," Chris said as he signed it, "I think someone defaced that before it broke."

"What do you mean?"

"Well, it had this weird Bible quote on it about killing babies or something like that."

"Don't try to make things up to get out of this. You still need to pay for it."

"I'm not . . . Okay. I've got to get going." He handed her the credit card slip.

"You are welcome to come back, young man."

"I will, I will. I just have to . . ."

Chris turned around and saw Karl's pickup going by. He ran outside, carefully avoiding bumping into anything. He ran after the truck, yelling and waving his arms.

"Hey! Karl! Stop! Hey!"

The pickup turned a corner and went out of sight. Chris groaned, rubbing his face with his hands.

Fuck it, I'm just going to walk back, he thought.

He mentally retraced the way they came in the pickup. He turned around and started walking that way. As he made his way back, he wondered where everyone was. He didn't see any other cars or people outside.

EIGHT

CHRIS WALKED ON THE side of the road. He checked his phone again. Agnes still hadn't responded. He remembered Karl's home phone number was still saved in his call history.

It's worth a try, he thought.

He selected the number and hit "call." He listened to the phone ring several times before he gave up and pressed the "end call" button.

Where is he? First Agnes, now her dad. What is going on?

He heard a car coming up behind him. He looked back and saw it was a police vehicle. It was slowing down. Chris stopped. The driver rolled his window down as it pulled up beside him, revealing a skinny man in his mid-thirties in a police uniform.

"You aren't hitchhiking, are you?" the policeman said.

"No, no. I'm just walking to where I'm staying."

"Good, soliciting rides is not only illegal here, it's dangerous. We've been searching all over the county for a couple of kids that went missing while hitching."

"I think I saw that on the news."

"I'll give you a ride to where you're going. Hop in."

"Oh, that's okay. It's pretty close to here."

"I insist. Besides, it's going to rain soon. Don't want to get caught out in that, do you?"

Chris shrugged and walked around to the other side. He climbed into the passenger's seat.

"I don't recognize you and I've seen a lot of the folks in this town." The policeman started the car. "Where are you from?"

"I'm from Iowa. Monk City, actually. I'm visiting because my girlfriend's mother passed and I'm here for the funeral."

"I'm sure sorry to hear that. What's your name?"

"Chris."

"Officer Matti Khorhonen, Elaine PD at your service. You can just call me Matt."

"Thanks a lot for the ride."

"So, why are you out walking around? Don't you have a car?"

"I had to leave that in Broken Bowl. The only road into town from there is closed, isn't it?"

"Oh, yes. I forgot about that. I don't leave town that often. You took the train into town?"

"Yeah. My girlfriend's dad was giving me a ride and then he had to go run around. He doesn't have a cell phone, so I can't call him."

"Sounds like you're not having a streak of good luck here."

"You don't know the half."

"How's your woman holding up?"

"That's the worst part. I haven't been able to find her since I got here, and she won't answer her phone."

"You haven't been able to get a hold of her at all?"

"She's answered some of my texts but that's about it. She said she was at a friend's place. I just came from there and she'd already left."

"That certainly is concerning."

The radio came on, giving a string of numbers. Matt grabbed the speaker microphone and responded.

"We've got a request for a 10-42 at the home on Musta Lane," the radio said.

"10-4. I'm on my way," Matt said.

"What's going on?" Chris said.

"Just a welfare check. An old lady lives alone there. Probably someone's grandma and they can't get out to see them. You mind if I stop and take it real quick? It's on the way."

"Sure, that's fine."

The police car turned down a gravel road. The woods surrounding them on both sides were thick enough to make the path darker. It was longer than Chris anticipated. He was starting to wonder where the house was. Then they finally came to it. It was a small wooden cottage sitting right where the forest became the beach on Lake Superior. It looked like it could use a new coat of paint. None of the lights were on, making it look abandoned. Behind it, Chris could see a small pier and a rowboat on the beach.

"I'll be back in a moment," Matt said.

Chris watched him get out of the car and walk up to the door. He knocked a few times. When no one answered, he knocked harder, shouting it was the police. Still no one answered. He tried the doorknob and it opened. He took his flashlight out of his belt and went inside.

Chris took his phone out of his pocket. He checked that he hadn't missed a text from Agnes. He hadn't. He texted Primavera.

"Everything still going smoothly?"

As soon as he hit send, a gun shot came from inside the home. Chris froze in his seat. He watched the door of the house until Matt threw it open and walked quickly toward the car. Chris saw he had his gun in his hand. He opened the door on Chris's side.

"Get out," he said.

"What the hell!" Chris said.

"Get out!"

He grabbed Chris by the arm and tried to pull him out, forgetting or ignoring that his seat belt was still on.

"Ouch! Stop it!" Chris said.

He fumbled to undo his seat belt and climbed out of the car.

"What is going on?" he said.

Matt pointed his gun at him. Chris threw his hands up and stood frozen with them above his head.

"Don't say anything," Matt said.

He started pointing directions to Chris.

"Here's what you're going to do. You're going to go down to that beach and walk that way. Keep going until you see a path to your left. That will take you to the house you're going to. Do not talk about this to anyone or I'll put a bullet in you."

Chris turned and ran toward the beach. He didn't look back. When he got to where the boat was resting, he headed in the direction Matt pointed. He kicked up sand as he ran. He glanced back when he thought he was far enough away. Realizing he was far enough away the house was nearly out of sight, he stopped to rest.

He sat down in the sand. He realized his phone was still gripped tightly in his hand and he was shaking. He thought about calling someone.

Who can I call that could help? he thought. *The police? They'd side with that guy. Fuck!*

He slid his phone into his pocket and held his face in his palm. He closed his eyes and listened to the waves of Lake Superior until he calmed down. He started as he felt something hit his head. He felt more come down on him and realized it was starting to rain. He stood up and headed back up the beach, picking up the pace as the rain started coming down harder.

NINE

CHRIS RAN UP THE path toward Karl's house as the rain beat down on him. He headed straight for the back door. To his relief, it was unlocked. He sighed as he shut the door behind him. He took his phone out of his wet pocket and set it on the kitchen counter. He took off his shoes and grabbed a dish cloth next to the sink.

"Hey, Karl! Are you here?" he called out as he wiped his arms and face.

There was no response.

"Karl?"

He walked through the dining room and the living room. Nobody was there. He tried checking downstairs rooms he hadn't been in yet. One was the downstairs bathroom, and it was unoccupied. One led to the basement and it was pitch-black at the bottom. The third one, which he suspected was Karl's bedroom, was locked. He knocked on the door.

"Karl? Are you in there?"

There was no answer. He walked to the front door and looked out the window next to it. Karl's pickup was still gone. He went upstairs. He went into the bathroom and stripped down to his boxers. He hung his wet clothes over the bathtub to dry. He walked back into the guest bedroom and changed into his pajamas. He stepped back out into the hall and looked around.

Something weird is going on here, he thought. *I'm going to get to the bottom of this bullshit.*

He looked into the first room to the right of the stairs. It looked like it belonged to a teenage girl from the early 2000s frozen in time. Posters of Eminem, Death Cab for Cutie, My Chemical Romance, and Fallout Boy were all over the wall. A desk on one side of the room had Hello Kitty dolls in bat, skeleton, and punk girl styles on the top shelf. Several pictures were taped to the side. A stack of notebooks was on it. A dresser with a mirror over it was on the other side of the room. It had some pictures in frames set on it. He stepped inside, taking in everything in the room.

This must have been Agnes's room, he thought. *It's exactly how I thought her room as a teenager would be. Why haven't they made any changes to it?*

The more he looked around the room, the more unsettled he felt.

Christ, Agnes is twenty-eight. This room has to have been like this for at least a decade.

He walked over to the dresser.

No dust. They've been cleaning it and leaving it exactly as is. What the hell?

He looked at the pictures. All of them were of a younger-looking Karl, a teenage Agnes, or what he assumed was her mother Susanna. He was surprised by how young she looked in the pictures. She could have been Agnes's older sister. They looked like a very happy family.

Maybe Sue dying really fucked both their heads up and that's why they're acting weird.

He checked the drawers on the dresser. All of them were empty. He walked over to the desk and examined the pictures on the side of it. Many of them were of Agnes as a teenager. A couple looked like school pictures. Others were of her in the woods, looking over a cliff in what was probably the Porcupine Mountains, or on the beach of Lake Superior in a bikini. In some of them, she was with her friends. Chris recognized one of the girls as a teenage Elaine, the one whose apartment he just got back from.

I wonder if any of these other girls are named Elaine too.

He opened one of the notebooks on the desk. He flipped through pages. It looked like a diary. The entries were dated from 2003 to 2005. However, he couldn't read anything else. Everything was written in a different language.

Must be in Finnish. I remember her telling me she spoke it. I didn't know she was that fluent though.

He checked one of the other notebooks. It looked like a book of poems, also in Finnish. Most of them were short, only a few lines, and had one-word titles like "Perkele," "Raiskaus," and "Veri."

Of course she wrote poetry. Then again, I wrote shitty songs when I was a teen, so I've got no room to talk.

He put the notebooks back how they were. He tried to open the drawer on the desk, but it was locked. As he thought about forcing it, he started when he heard a soft sound in the distance. He froze in place until he realized it was his phone. He suddenly remembered he left it in the kitchen.

He headed out of the room, shutting the door behind him, and down the stairs into the kitchen. He grabbed his phone off the counter. He'd gotten a text from Primavera.

"It's going good! Got the album and customer info like you told me to. How's Agnes doing?"

He sent a text back.

"Something really messed up is going on with this town. I'm pretty sure I saw a cop murder an old lady just a little bit ago. If I don't respond after a day, call someone to come look for me."

He sighed and slid the phone into the pocket of his pajama pants.

I hate to worry her, he thought. *But I'd rather not take a chance.*

He went to the front door and looked outside. Karl's truck was still gone. He closed the door, making sure it was locked, and headed back up the stairs. He went into the room across the hall from Agnes's. He started when the door suddenly stopped and made a loud, metallic clatter.

He froze for a moment before peeking around the door. It had hit a pile of folding chairs on the floor. He edged into the room and moved the chairs. He looked around the room. There were boxes all over the floor, as well as an ironing board, a bed frame, a couple fans, and some picture frames. Against the walls were bookcases. A couple of them were empty, others were full of books.

Chris walked over to the nearest bookcase, stepping over all the junk on the floor. Its three middle rows were filled with hardcover books and the rest were empty. The top row was all red books, the middle white, and the bottom blue. There were no titles on the spines. When he pulled out one of the books he saw there was no title on the cover either.

When he opened one of the red books, he saw it was a sex education book from 1968. He laughed as he looked through the illustrations and read some of the text. It was clearly made for a rather prudish audience. He wondered if Agnes's family only bought it for the color or if they used it to teach the kids in their family.

He put the red book back and opened one of the white books. Like Agnes's notebooks, it was written all in Finnish.

I wish I could read this, he thought.

He pulled out his phone and tried to bring up Google. The loading circle just kept spinning before he gave up and put the phone back in his pocket.

If I could just get the internet, I could translate it.

He put the white book back and pulled out a blue one. It was from a set of encyclopedias from 1975.

I haven't seen an encyclopedia since elementary school. Either they're pack rats or this set has sentimental value.

He put the encyclopedia back in the bookcase. He bent down and opened the box on the floor. There wasn't much in the box. A couple of old Christmas cards, some pens, and a few knickknacks. One of them looked exactly like the Precious Moments figurine he broke in the store earlier. He picked it up and looked at the tablet the angel was holding. It looked like the paint with the Bible quote, or whatever had been on it, had faded off almost completely. There was nothing but a couple of flecks of paint indicating something had been written on it.

As he set the figurine back in the box, he noticed a keychain with a rubber attachment shaped like the number one. He picked it up and saw there was a key attached to it. He looked at the key. The initials of the brand on it were the same as the ones on the desk drawer in the room across the hall.

Chris took the key into Agnes's room and went straight to the desk. He put the key in the lock. The locked clicked and the drawer opened.

I'm surprised that key was there. Maybe Agnes lost it?

Inside the drawer, there was a pile of what looked like letters. Like the notebooks, they were written all in Finnish. However, he could tell they seemed to be addressed to Agnes from Elaine. He wondered which Elaine was writing. The answer seemed to come in a Polaroid picture that fell out of the pile.

He bent down and picked it up. It was a picture of a teenage Agnes and the Elaine who tried to seduce him earlier. Both of them seemed to be naked. Elaine lay on Agnes's breasts. Elaine's arm was extended out of the frame, suggesting she was the holding the camera to take the picture. The darkness around them made it obvious the flash from the camera was the only light.

Agnes looked how he expected her too. She had swooped bangs, heavy wing mascara, and black lipstick. Looking at Elaine made him extremely uncomfortable. She looked exactly like his sister, Amy, at the age sixteen, from her haircut to the way she wore her makeup. She even had the same smile. Before he knew it, he realized he was staring at her naked breasts and imagining the intimate situation she'd obviously been in before the picture was taken. His penis quickly got hard.

He shoved the photo back in the pile of letters, put them back in the drawer, and locked it. He slid the key into his pocket and quickly walked to the bathroom. He splashed cold water on his face and looked at himself in the mirror.

"What the hell is wrong with you?" he said out loud. "Why the hell are you thinking this shit? Is it this town? Is it messing with your head?"

He wiped his face on a towel hung by the sink.

"I need to calm down. I need to relax a little bit."

He went down the stairs into the living room. He sat on the couch and turned on the TV. An episode of *Murder, She Wrote* was just starting. He sat and watched. He tried to get invested in the story, but his thoughts kept turning back to the picture.

Agnes and Elaine were definitely more than friends. Those had to have been love letters. They must have meant a lot for her to keep them. Was Agnes over there sleeping with her when I arrived? Is that why she's avoiding me? But why is Elaine trying to sleep with me? Where the fuck is Agnes? Where the fuck is Karl? Fuck!

As he sat there, the events of the day started catching up with him and he suddenly felt very, very tired. He lay down on the couch, letting himself drift off to sleep without bothering to turn the TV off.

TEN

***CHRIS WAKES TO A** slap across the face. He realizes he's sitting up and tied to a chair. His pants are gone. He looks up and sees Agnes. "You pig!" she says. "I saw the way you were looking at Elaine and Amy! Your sister! Are you that horny that any girl will do?" She slaps him again. He tries to speak. "No!" he says. "It's not like that!" He looks around and sees he's in an empty room. Only him, the chair he was sitting on, and Agnes. Not even a door. "Oh yeah? How is it then?" Agnes says. There is a sound like a door opening. What he thinks are two Amys are suddenly standing against the wall. He looks closer and realizes that one of them is Elaine. "Look at that!" Agnes says. "Even now you're looking at them instead of me!" "No! No!" he says. "If you want them so fucking bad you can have them!" Agnes says. Amy and Elaine approach him. Amy balls a fist and punches him in the face. He feels his teeth cut the inside of his cheek. He spits blood onto the floor. "What is wrong with you?" Amy says. "I always knew you were fucked up. You want to fuck your own sister? That's so disgusting!" She punches him again. He feels the blood rushing to his cock. Elaine laughs. "Look at this!" she says. "Not only is he an incest loving pervert, he's a masochist!" "Stop, please," he says. "Jesus Christ," Amy says. "You're so disgusting!" His cock is rock hard. His face flushes with humiliation. Amy pulls out the tie holding up her ponytail. She wraps it tightly around the base of his scrotum. She pulls her panties off and lifts her skirt up. "This is what you want, isn't it?" she says. "I'll give you what you want, you nasty little shit, but you don't get to cum." Amy sits on his cock. It slides into her pussy. She's soaking wet. Chris closes his eyes tightly. "Amy, don't, please," he says. He opens his eyes. Amy is Elaine.*

Agnes is gone. "Does that feel good?" Elaine says. "Get off," he says. "Please get off." Elaine giggles. "I plan to," she says. She starts fucking herself on his cock. "Oh fuck!" he says. "I knew you'd love it. You fucking pervert!" Amy says. Elaine is Amy. "You'd better enjoy it. You're going to be a dildo for me. Dildos don't cum, so you don't get to!" She fucks herself faster on him. He feels himself about to cum. The band around his scrotum prevents him from cumming. "Ouch! Fuck!" he says. "Please let me cum!" Amy is Elaine again. "Oh, poor baby," she says. "It hurts, doesn't it?" He nods. "Too fucking bad! "Amy says. Elaine is Amy again. "Hurt, you fucking pig!" Chris clenches his teeth. He feels himself about to cry from the pain.

ELEVEN

CHRIS WOKE UP AND sat up on the couch. Even though his pajama pants were loose, he still felt as if his erection was going to tear through them. He didn't look at the TV or what time it was. Like he was on autopilot, he went straight back up the stairs, into Agnes's room, and opened the drawer. He dug out the photo and headed to the bathroom. He locked the door behind him and stripped naked. He sat on the toilet and furiously masturbated as he looked at the picture of Agnes and Elaine.

In his fantasy, his sister Amy and Elaine were the same person. She sat on his face while Agnes fucked herself on his cock. Both of them insulted him, saying how disgusting he was. Amy/Elaine put all her weight on his face, making it impossible to breathe.

It didn't take long before he came so hard, it hit under his chin. He sat there on the toilet, his torso covered in his semen, trying to catch his breath. When he came to his senses, he nearly tore the picture in half but stopped himself before he did.

No, no. I can't tear it, he thought. *If she finds it's gone, Agnes will know what I did and that will make it way worse.*

He set the picture on the sink and climbed into the shower. He scrubbed himself with his teeth clenched.

Jesus Christ. I'm so fucked up. It's the town. It has to be.

He quickly got out and dried himself off. He dressed himself in the clothes he had hung out to dry, transferring his phone and the drawer key to his jeans' pocket. He returned the picture to the drawer and threw his pajamas on his bed in his room.

No way I'm getting back to sleep now.

He checked the time on his phone. It was almost eight a.m. He also saw that the phone was down to five percent. He walked back downstairs and into the living room. As he plugged in his phone, he noticed the introduction to Pastor Toivo's show on the TV. He sat down and watched.

"Good morning, brothers and sisters in Christ," Pastor Toivo said. "I am Pastor Toivo and thank you for joining me again. Today's reading from the Bible is from Genesis, verses 18-19."

The pastor began to recite the story of Sodom and Gomorrah.

Oh, great, Chris thought. *He's going to say some backwards shit about gay people, isn't he? I don't know if that's better or worse than his rape and murder fantasies.*

He talked about how God came to Abraham and told him he planned to burn Sodom and Gomorrah unless righteous men were found. God sent two angels to meet Abraham's nephew Lot in the city. While staying with him, men gathered around his house demanding he bring the angels out so they could have sex with them. Lot offered his two daughters instead. The men refused and attempted to break into Lot's house, threatening to do even worse to him.

Despite knowing where he was likely going with the sermon, he found the way the pastor read it to be riveting. He had a calming and engaging voice, which seemed to come naturally. He could understand why the man was on TV, even in spite of his obvious mental problems.

The pastor continued, telling how God struck the men with blindness and instructed Lot's family to leave. As they left, God rained fire and brimstone, destroying the city. Lot's wife ignored the orders not to look back at the burning city and became a pillar of salt. Lot and his daughters escaped into the nearby mountains. His daughters, believing there would be no men around to carry their father's seed, got him drunk and slept with him. The preacher ended by saying his daughters became pregnant by him. The pastor closed his Bible as he finished the story.

Oh, Christ. I forgot about the daughter fucking at the end of that story. That's a theme with him, isn't it?

"Now, this is a well-known story from the Bible for a reason. We live in very wicked times. I would argue these times are more wicked than Sodom and Gomorrah in those days. We even derive the term 'sodomy' from this story. Now, many have used it as a term for the sin of homosexuality, but it is not just for that. Any sexual act which does not produce children is a grave sin in the eyes of the Lord."

Chris made a jerk-off gesture with his hand.

Oh, wait. Guess that's a sin too.

"Just as God demands sacrifice, blood, and fire to cleanse away the wicked, he demands we create more worshipers for him. God's commandment to go forth and multiply is of the utmost importance. Lot's daughters understood this and, knowing they had no other men, turned to their beloved father to bear children. Our wicked times considers this taboo, but it is a perfectly moral thing for a daughter to honor her father by taking his seed."

Yep. This pervert likes his daughter fucking. Jesus. What is wrong with this town? Why would it let him on TV?

"My daughter Elaine knows this well. I myself have taught her to take my seed even before she was capable of bearing children. We now happily have three children together; two girls and one boy. We plan to have as many as possible."

"Wait?" Chris said. "What!"

"I've also been teaching my granddaughters how to take a man's seed. They'll make wonderful mothers when—"

Chris shut off the TV. He sat there in disbelief.

"Fuck," he said. "I wouldn't have thought it could get any worse."

His phone rang. He jumped off the couch and hit his leg on the coffee table. He rubbed his shin, quietly cursing to himself as he limped over to where his phone was plugged in. It was a call from Primavera.

"Hello," he said as he answered.

There was a quiet woman's voice on the other end. He didn't catch what it said. He felt a tinge of dread in his stomach.

"What? Who is this?" he said.

"It's me, Pri. I just got your text," Primavera said quietly. "Is everything okay there?

"Not really."

He sighed in relief.

"Why are you talking so low?"

"I spent the night at Alex's place and he's still asleep. What's wrong? Did you really see a cop kill someone?"

"You'll need to speak up. The signal here is shit. And that's not exactly what I saw."

Chris recounted what happened with the police officer who called himself Matt.

"And that's not all that's happened," he said. "I haven't seen Agnes since I got here. Her dad disappeared too. I haven't seen him since yesterday. To top it all off, there's a really crazy pastor on the local TV here. It sounds hard to believe, but I seriously heard him talking about molesting his daughter and getting her pregnant."

"Oh my god!" Primavera said. "Have you tried getting out of town? It sounds like you need to."

"I'm going to try. I'm going to try to find out when the next train to Broken Bowl is, then I'll figure it out from there."

"There must be something wrong with Agnes if you can't find her. That's not at all like her to disappear."

"I know. I thought it was her grief over losing her mother, but there's too much else going on."

"Okay. Come back safe. Like you said, I'll call the police if I don't hear back from you after a while."

"I don't know what they'll do, but thanks a lot."

"Of course!"

"I'll let you know when I'm back in Broken Bowl."

"Okay. Talk to you later. Be safe."

"I'll try to."

He hung up the phone. He walked outside and looked around. Karl's truck was still nowhere to be seen. He noticed there was a newspaper by the door. He opened it and found one of the headlines read, "Local Woman Found Dead in Her Home."

"Officer Matti Khorhonen was called by Graveraet resident John Koskinen to do a wellness check on his mother, Elaine Koskinen, who resides in Elaine. According to Officer Khorhonen, he arrived at her home in the afternoon and no one answered the door. He entered the home, finding the door unlocked, and searched for the elderly woman. Upon locating her on the bathroom floor, he found her to have passed away. Upon seeing her, Officer Khorhonen panicked, drew his firearm, and accidentally discharged it at her body. He called for an ambulance. After a brief examination by paramedics, it was determined that she had been dead for at least two days. Officer Khorhonen was reprimanded for his reaction, but otherwise has been cleared of any wrongdoing. Elaine Koskinen is survived by her son, John Koskinen, and her stepdaughter, Anne Koskinen."

That sounds like complete bullshit, Chris thought. *There's no way he knew she was dead from his reaction. He had to have killed her. They must be covering up. But, then again, did he have any reason to kill her?*

He stood with the front door open, listening to the sounds of Lake Superior.

Fuck it. I'm just going to have some breakfast and then head to the train station.

Chris made a breakfast of coffee and Cheerios he found in the kitchen cupboard. He read the paper as he ate. There was very little in it he found that grabbed his attention. Apart from the Officer Khorhonen story and a brief update about two missing teenagers from Ironhorse, everything that wasn't national news from the Associated Press was almost entirely fluff, stories about kids playing Red Rover at the park and a renovation being done at the city hall. He read the story about the missing teenagers carefully. He had blown it off when he heard it on the news but now thought it could be a clue as to what was going on.

Two high school students on summer vacation had tried to hitchhike to the Porcupine Mountains to go camping, having apparently lied to their families and saying they were driving up with a group of friends. They were last seen by a truck driver who gave them a ride into Broken Bowl and had not been heard from for over a month. The families were now offering a thousand-dollar reward for any information leading to them being found. He briefly wondered if those kids ended up here in Elaine.

He finished his breakfast and washed his dishes, mentally trying to retrace how to get to the train station from Karl's house. He pulled out his phone and tried to bring up Google. To his surprise, it loaded right away. However, when he tried to search for information on the trains in Elaine, it stayed on the loading circle until finally bringing up an "unable to connect" page.

Why does this fucking thing work sometimes and not others up here? I could talk to Pri just fine, but now I can't bring up a simple search.

He explored the house, trying to find some kind of road map or train schedule, but there was nothing. He found an umbrella in the closet and grabbed it in case it started raining again.

Okay, I'm pretty sure it was a straight drive to the home from the station. If I just take a walk up the road I should reach it.

He packed everything he had into his backpack and suitcase and headed out. He put in his earbuds and started listening to the playlist on his phone as he walked. He wasn't very far up the road when it began to drizzle. He put up the umbrella, listening to the rain hit it along with the sound of "Roses" by Outkast playing in his ears.

After walking up the road for a while, he took a break. He set his suitcase down and sat on it. It was soaking wet from the rain. "The Jeep Song" by The Dresden Dolls was playing. He took his phone out and checked the time. It was already almost ten. He looked up and down the road. He hadn't seen any cars since he set out. He wasn't sure if that was a good or a bad sign at this point.

He stood and headed back up the road. After some time, he spotted the gravel parking lot on the other side of the road. He jogged across the street and the lot up to the door of the train station. He tried to open the door, but it wouldn't budge. He checked the door and realized a faded red 'Closed' sign was hanging on it. He tried looking in the windows, but all of them had the blinds closed. He checked his phone again. It was almost ten-thirty. He leaned against the wall beside the door.

I'll wait here until it's open. Maybe the trains don't run until the afternoon.

He pulled up the messages he sent to Agnes. She still hadn't gotten in contact. He thought about sending her a harsh rebuke or demanding an explanation. Instead, he sent her a single sentence.

"I'm going back home."

He stood by the door and waited, listening to "Into the Lens" by Yes.

Chris continued standing by the door, waiting for someone to open the station. He paced back and forth in front of it, stretched out, and listened to more songs on his phone. When the rain let up, he jogged a couple laps around the gravel lot. When he checked his phone again, it was almost one p.m.

Christ. Is it closed today?

He sighed and grabbed his suitcase. He left the station and

headed back down the road toward Karl's house.

I'll come back later.

Chris arrived back at the house. There were still no cars out front. To his relief, the door was also still unlocked. He took his suitcase and backpack back up to the guest bedroom. He sat down on the bed and thought about what he should do next.

I guess I'll go into town and ask around when the next train is going to be.

He lay back on the bed, his arms spread out.

Fuck. I'm tired from all that walking. I'll take a quick nap and then head into town.

Before he knew it, he drifted off.

TWELVE

CHRIS IS WALKING ON *the beach with Agnes. Agnes is pregnant. Lake Superior sounds more beautiful than ever to him. He feels happy. They walk until they come to a dock on the beach. It leads to a church on the lake. Agnes pulls him toward the church. He hesitates but follows. They enter. The church is dark except for the light coming through the stained-glass windows. Agnes begins taking her clothes off. He tries to ask her what she's doing. The words catch in his throat. He realizes he can't move. Agnes strips naked. Her stomach is heavy with child. She walks to the altar and climbs onto it. As she lies there, Pastor Toivo appears seemingly out of nowhere. He reaches between her legs. He says her pussy feels so hot. Chris tries to run to him. He wants to beat the pastor. He still can't move. He still can't speak. The pastor picks up a butcher knife. He says a prayer and shoves the knife into Agnes's vagina. Instead of screaming, she moans like it feels good. He runs the knife through her, cutting her stomach open. She cries out as if having an orgasm. She twitches then stops moving. The pastor pulls the baby out of the bloody wound. He says it's a healthy girl. He wraps Agnes's body in the cloth on the altar and pulls her off onto the floor. Chris wants to scream and cry, but he can't. The pastor puts a new cloth on the altar. Chris feels someone pushing him. His feet move on their own. They strip off his clothes and push him onto the altar. He sees Amy standing above him. She mocks him for having an erection. She grabs it. She strokes it until he cums on to his chest and stomach. She lifts the butcher knife above him, still wet with Agnes's blood. As she brings it down, a scream finally escapes from his mouth.*

THIRTEEN

CHRIS'S EYES SHOT OPEN as he gasped. He sat up, breathing heavy. He looked around and cradled his head in his hands.

"Jesus fucking Christ," he said. "The dreams are getting worse."

He felt a sticky wetness. For a moment, he thought he was actually bleeding. Then he realized it was in the crotch of his pants.

"You've got to be fucking kidding me," he said, feeling the wetness. "I came from that disgusting shit?"

He stripped off his boxers and jeans and threw them in the corner. He grabbed different ones from his suitcase and changed into them. He checked his phone, it was almost five p.m.

Damn. I slept longer than I wanted to, he thought. *This town is fucking with my head. I have to get out of here.*

Chris walked down the sidewalk in downtown Elaine, the umbrella hanging at this side. The rain had stopped. The town felt just as empty as before. He checked his phone. It was half past five. Even as small a town as this should have had more people around at this time. He saw a few cars parked in the street and the occasional person in the window of the stores, but it still seemed eerily quiet and empty as if they were just props to keep him from believing the town was completely abandoned. The gray sheet of clouds overhead didn't help.

He came to a building with a sign that read "Raincloud Café." He realized he hadn't eaten since breakfast and headed inside. A bell above the door rang as he entered. As he expected, there were no other customers, but he could see people walking around in the kitchen in the back. He took a seat at a table. He looked around. It looked like every mom and pop diner he'd been in before. A blond middle-aged woman wearing an apron approached his table. When she got close enough, he could see a nametag on her shirt that said, "Elaine."

Of course, he thought.

She set a menu down in front of him. In the transparent plastic sheets was off-white paper with the words "Raincloud Café" in a simple font with nothing else. When he flipped it over, the selection of drinks and desserts was just a simple list. There weren't even logos for the pop like most other menus had.

"Can I get you something to drink to start off with?" Elaine said.

"A Diet Coke, please," Chris said.

She nodded and headed back to the kitchen. He looked through the menu. It was all typical diner food except for the venison burger and the pasties. The waitress came back and set his Coke in front of him.

"What can I get for you?"

"The venison burger sounds good. Can I get that with a side of fries?"

"I'm so sorry. There's a do not eat advisory on deer. They've been getting sick around here and we're not supposed to serve that. Anything else?"

"Oh. I guess I'll have the two pasty meal then."

"Great choice. I'll have it right out for you."

When the waitress left, he got up and grabbed a newspaper from the stand sitting next to the door. He flipped through it. He couldn't find anything regarding a warning about deer in the area.

Maybe I'm being too paranoid, he thought, *but I'm starting to suspect everyone in this town is fucking with me.*

He returned to his table. Not long after, the waitress brought his pasties out to him.

"I hope you enjoy!"

"It looks delicious. Hey, do you know when the next train out of town is?"

"Train?"

"You know, the train to Broken Bowl?"

"There's a train here?"

"That's how I got into town."

"Why didn't you take the road?"

"The road's closed, isn't it?"

"Oh, yeah. I think I might have heard that somewhere. I'm sorry. I don't pay much attention to the news or anything. I'm so busy here that I don't know much about going in and out of town."

Chris looked around the empty diner.

"I can see why," he said. "Thanks anyway."

"Enjoy your pasties!"

When the waitress walked away, he started stabbing at the pasties. Finding no razors or needles like he vaguely suspected he would, he took a forkful of it and smelled it. It seemed to be fine.

I must be getting too paranoid, he thought. *Fuck it. I'm starving. If I die of poisoning, I die.*

He took a bite and didn't taste anything off. They weren't as good as the ones Karl made, but they were still delicious. He finished them quickly. The waitress came back and took his plate.

"You must have been hungry," she said.

"Very."

"Anything else I can get you?"

"No, thanks. Can I get the check? I got to get out of here."

The waitress set a handwritten bill in front of him and took off back toward the kitchen. He left the money in cash on the table with a three-dollar tip.

She didn't try to poison me, he thought as he went out the door. *That's worth a tip under these circumstances.*

He walked up the streets. The sense that the town was a fake, like a big movie set, returned. It was just as empty as before.

Watch, I start puking blood and shitting my pants here in a little bit.

As he walked along, he felt the pasties settle in his stomach, but nothing out of the ordinary. Soon, he came back to the building with Elaine and Maija's Gifts and the door that led to Elaine's apartment.

Elaine might be willing to help out.

He remembered the picture with Agnes and changed his mind. He headed into the gift store instead. The old woman from the other day was standing at the counter reading a book. A gray tabby cat was sleeping on the counter. He approached her. She looked up at him, marking her place in the book and setting it down. Out of the corner of his eye, he saw the book was a black hardcover with no writing on it.

"Welcome back, young man," the woman said. "How can I help you?"

"Yeah, uh, do you know anything about the train here?"

"The train?"

"Yeah, the one that goes to Broken Bowl."

"Yes, I know. What about it?"

"Do you know the next time it leaves?"

"I don't. Did you go to the train station?"

"It's closed today."

"I don't know anything about it. I haven't used it in a very long time. My husband is here. He might know. He's traveled out of town more often than I have."

The old woman opened a door behind her and leaned in.

"Honey," she said, "would you come in here for a minute?"

After a moment, the man emerged from the back. Chris quickly recognized him as Pastor Toivo. He froze. His mind raced, trying to process the fact that the man who drooled over raping his daughter on TV was standing right in front of him. He was pulled back to reality when he realized the pastor was saying something to him.

"Young man," the pastor said, "are you okay? You wanted to know when the next train to Broken Bowl is?"

"Uh, just a second."

Chris pulled out his phone and looked at it, pretending to check a text he hadn't received.

"Oh, uh, I have to go. It's an emergency."

Before the pastor could say anything else, Chris turned around and quickly walked out of the store. He walked a couple blocks, looking back to make sure nobody was following him.

"Holy shit," he said. "Literally. I wasn't expecting to see that sick fuck."

He sighed.

What do I do now? he thought.

He looked around and realized there was what looked like a bar called "Henri's" across the street.

Well, I always went to the taverns for information in my middle-school D&D campaigns. Why not here?

FOURTEEN

CHRIS WALKED INTO HENRI'S. Like the Raincloud Café looked like every diner he'd eaten in, Henri's looked like every dive bar he'd drank in. The only person there was the bartender. The jukebox next to the door caught his eye. It still used CDs instead of being a digital one with a touchscreen that even the shittiest dives in Monk City had now. "Can't Break It to My Heart" by Tracy Lawrence was playing on it. He flipped through the selections. It was mostly country and older rock music. Alan Jackson, Tim McGraw, Def Leppard, Kenny Rogers, Whitesnake, Willie Nelson, Led Zeppelin, Johnny Cash, and Aerosmith were all there. It wasn't even in alphabetical order as if whoever put the selections in couldn't be bothered. He put in a dollar and selected "The Evil That Men Do" by Iron Maiden. He hit the button to return change and grabbed the three quarters that returned. He walked up to the bar and took a seat.

"Hey, what can I get you?" the bartender said.

"You got Busch Light?"

"Yep."

The bartender reached into the fridge behind the bar and set a tallboy in front of him.

"Two dollars," the bartender said.

Chris set a ten on the bar.

"Keep it. I'm going to want another one after this."

"Thanks, buddy."

"Hey, do you know anything about the train to Broken Bowl?"

"Been years since I've taken it. What about it?"

"Do you know when the next one leaves?"

"Can't say I do. You trying to get to Broken Bowl?"

"I am. Is there still construction on the road here?"

"Last I heard there is. You tried asking at the station?"

"I went there earlier, and it was closed. Do you have a phone number for them?"

The bartender pointed to a pay phone with a phone book hanging from it by a chain.

"You're free to take a look in there."

This town really is two decades behind, Chris thought as he got up.

He flipped through the phone book until he found an entry for Lake Superior Passenger Railway. He dialed the number on his phone. As he expected, it just kept ringing and ringing with no answer. He hung up and saved the number in his contacts.

I'll try them tomorrow morning, he thought.

He took his seat at the bar. "The Night the Lights Went Out in Georgia" by Reba McEntire ended on the jukebox and the Iron Maiden song he had selected started. A show was playing on the TV hanging on the wall. A man in a mask and dressed in all black was riding a horse. It took him a moment to realize who the character was.

Oh, Zorro, he thought. *My dad used to watch this all the time.*

Chris sat sipping his beer and watching the show, following the dialogue in the closed captioning. During a commercial break he got up to use the bathroom. It looked cleaner than it smelled. He breathed through his mouth as he went up to the urinal. While he was emptying his bladder, he looked over at the bathroom stall. There was a large and crudely drawn but detailed drawing of a woman's torso with large breasts and thick pubic hair. A dotted line was down the center of the belly with the words "cut here" scrawled next to it. The stumps of the arms, legs, and neck were drawn in a way to suggest the graffiti artist intended the limbs and head to appear amputated rather than simply undrawn.

He shivered as he looked at the drawing and quickly finished, heading back to his seat without washing his hands. He quickly finished his beer and ordered another one. He went back to watching *Zorro*, trying to calm his nerves. He was pulled out of his focus on the TV by a hand on his shoulder. He started and dropped his beer. The can spilled on the bar and rolled behind it. The bartender cursed and picked it up.

Chris's head shot toward the hand's owner. The police officer, Matt, was standing over him and grinning. He was wearing a flannel shirt and jeans instead of his police uniform. He took his hand off Chris's shoulder and held it up.

"Hey, sorry about that!" Matt said. "Didn't mean to scare you."

"Uh, no, it's cool," Chris said. "I was already kind of on edge."

"I always come here after I get off duty. Didn't expect to see you here. You ever find your girl?"

"Uh, no. I haven't heard from her or her dad."

"Oh, that's rough. Came here to drown your sorrows?"

"Well, uh, yeah, basically."

"Sorry about what happened last time. That wasn't the first time I saw a dead body, but I wasn't expecting one and being by myself I just panicked, you know?"

"Oh, yeah. I saw the article in the newspaper."

"I mean, you don't think I just shot some old lady for no reason, do you?"

Chris wasn't sure if it was his nerves, but he swore he heard a threatening tone in the question.

"No, no," he said. "Of course not."

"Let me buy you another beer," Matt said. "I feel bad I made you spill yours."

Matt ordered two more Busch Lights as well as two shots of Fireball. He picked up one of the shot glasses and raised it.

"To life!" Matt said.

Chris hesitated for a moment and then grabbed the other glass. He raised it as well.

"To life," he said.

They clinked their glasses, tapped them on the bar, and threw them back. Chris felt the burn in his throat and shook his head. Matt laughed.

"What's the matter?" he said. "You a light-weight?"

"I am these days," Chris said. "My girlfriend hates liquor, so it's been a while since I've had it."

"Guess you can enjoy a little freedom from her."

"To be honest, my patience has run out and I'm leaving as soon as I can. You know when the next train to Broken Bowl is?"

"Should be tomorrow afternoon. They close every

Wednesday."

"Oh, so that's why it wasn't open when I went there."

"Tonight's your going away party then. Hey, Henri, can we get two more shots of Fireball?"

"I've only been here a couple days. Besides, I don't want to be too hung over to make the train."

"You'll have plenty of time. It doesn't leave until like four or five in the afternoon. It sounds like you've been through some shit and need to let a little loose."

Chris shrugged and took the shot. It was easier to get down this time.

"You play pool?" Matt said.

"Yeah. I'm not great at it though."

"I'll go easy on you. Loser buys the next round. What do you say?"

"Sure, why not?"

They headed over to the pool table. Matt set up the balls and Chris agreed to let him break. Matt didn't sink any on his turn. Chris, however, was able to sink two solids on his turn. Matt laughed.

"You trying to hustle me?" he said.

Chris laughed as well.

"Nah. I'm seriously not good at this game, but I guess I had a stroke of luck."

Chris's luck continued, and he won the game quickly. Matt patted him on the back and congratulated him. Chris was starting to warm up to him.

Maybe I was wrong about my suspicions of him.

"Welp, this one's on me," Matt said. "Want the same? Another shot too?"

"Yeah. I'll take another Busch Light. Fuck it. Another Fireball too."

"That's the spirit!"

While Matt was getting the drinks, Chris went back over to the jukebox. "Indian Outlaw" by Tim McGraw was playing. He scrunched up his face. He put a dollar in the slot. He selected "Proud Mary" by Creedence Clearwater Revival, "Born in the USA" by Bruce Springsteen, "All My Rowdy Friends Have Settled Down" by Hank Williams Jr., and "The Road Goes on Forever" by The Highwaymen. He went back over to the bar where Matt was waiting for him. They threw back their shots. Chris was starting to feel a little tipsy.

"How about another game?" Matt said.

"I'm apparently a god and didn't know it, so sure."

Matt laughed.

"Don't get cocky. There's only one god, and he sure ain't you."

FIFTEEN

AS MATT AND CHRIS played their game, more people came into the bar. Most of them were obviously blue-collar workers getting off from their job. They still wore their overalls and work boots. A few of them came with what were apparently their girlfriends or wives. The bar was starting to resemble more of a real place than the facade it felt like when he first walked in. As he drank more and mingled with the other patrons, he started to forget about his paranoia about the town. In the back of his mind, he was starting to believe there was only a problem with a select few in the town, Agnes and her father being among them.

As the evening turned to night he was feeling good and intoxicated. He kept making trips to the jukebox to select more songs. Matt ribbed him for it.

"What are you, some kind of music snob?" he said, laughing.

"Hey, I own a record store," Chris said. His speech was starting to slur. "It's part of my job."

"People still buy CDs? I thought everyone got stuff online."

"Nah, man. I sell mostly actual records. Since everyone streams shit now, people who collect went back to them."

"Actual vinyl records? People still buy those? Seriously? Even my dad sold his records for CDs back in the 90s."

"I make a good living, so I can definitely tell you people buy them."

As he was talking with Matt, he spotted a woman coming in to the bar. It took him a moment to realize it was Elaine. The one he'd seen in the picture with Agnes. In a sober mindset, he'd be afraid of her and would leave the bar right away. However, enough alcohol had soaked his brain that he went straight to thinking about how great her tits had looked in the picture and the flash of her pussy he'd seen when he was at her place. The tight t-shirt and jean shorts she was wearing just enforced those thoughts. The nagging sense of how gross it was that she looked exactly like his sister was in the back of his mind, but it was so muted by the booze it may as well not even have been there. His base instincts were in control. When she spotted him, she smiled and waved.

"Hey, I'll be back in just a minute," Chris said. "I'm going to go talk to someone I know."

Matt looked behind him and saw Elaine. He turned back to Chris, grinned, and patted him on the shoulder.

"All right, I see," he said. "Go get her, buddy."

Chris walked over to Elaine.

"Hey!" Chris said to her. "I didn't expect to see you here."

"Same here. That seems to be a pattern with us. How is Agnes doing?"

"You're not going to believe this, but I still haven't found her. And her dad's gone missing, too."

"You're kidding me. Really? That's not like them at all."

"I know it's not like Agnes. I'm pissed at her, to be honest. I'm thinking she's avoiding me on purpose."

"Oh, I'm sure she's not! There's probably an explanation for it."

"I'm leaving tomorrow on the first train I can catch. Tonight, I'm just getting it off my mind. Can I buy you a drink?"

"I'd love that!"

Chris and Elaine walked up to the bar. Elaine ordered a rum and Coke and pointed to a table in the corner.

"Why don't we sit over there?" she said. "It's a little more quiet and private."

They took their seats at the table. "Friends in Low Places" by Garth Brooks was playing on the jukebox.

"So, why are you leaving tomorrow?" Elaine said. "Are you that mad at Agnes and her dad?"

"It's not just that. I can't get a hold of them at all, so I don't see the point in sticking around."

"You could stick around for a little bit. There's plenty to do here."

"Oh yeah? In this town? What is there to do?"

Elaine grinned.

"You just need to know where to look."

Chris and Elaine sat there talking, flirting, and drinking. Elaine revealed that she worked at a CPA that did the taxes for most of the businesses in town, that she lived there all her life, and that she hadn't been out of town since she moved back from Grand River where she had gone to college at Hobbes University. It seemed odd to him she had stayed in this isolated little town, but then he realized this trip was the first time he'd left Monk City in years. Occasionally, the image of the photo would come back into his head. At one point in his inebriated state, he nearly let a question about it slip, but he managed to catch himself. At that point, he knew he needed to grab some water and sober up a little bit.

"Had enough?" Elaine said as he returned to the table with the glass of water.

"I don't want to get a hangover and I need to walk back to the house."

"Speaking of, what time is it?"

Chris checked his phone.

"Wow," he said. "It's already nine-thirty."

"I do need to work tomorrow morning. Why don't you come sober up at my apartment before you head home?"

"Sounds good to me."

Chris and Elaine headed for the door. Chris put his arm around her waist. She smiled at him and moved closer to him, putting her head on his shoulder. As they walked away, Chris could hear "Heat of the Moment" by Asia starting on the jukebox.

SIXTEEN

AS CHRIS AND ELAINE trudged up the stairs leading to her apartment, the only thing on his mind was the feeling of her ass in her jean shorts which he'd been copping not at all discrete feels of as they were walking. She giggled, seeming to be delighted by them. As soon as the door closed, his arms were around her and his lips against hers. He squeezed her ass in his hands as she ran hers up and down his back. He held her tight, his hard-on pressing against her through his jeans. She kissed his neck, sucking on it until she left a hickey.

She broke from him and took his hand, leading him into her bedroom. Soon, their clothes were on the floor. He admired her naked body for a brief moment before grabbing her and forcing her on to the bed. She gasped with a mix of surprise and delight. He pinned her down, kissing her, grabbing her tits, and pulling on her nipples.

Two voices in his head were yammering at him. One was saying, "Your sister, dude! She looks like your sister!" That, to his own deep disgust, just made him hornier. He knew he'd hate himself for it when he was sober in the morning. The other voice of rationality had a better point.

"Hey, do you have a condom?" he whispered to her.

"It's okay," she said. "I'm on birth control."

She reached down and grabbed his hard cock, roughly jerking it. She pulled him, forcing him between her legs. He didn't fight, pushing himself inside her. He groaned as he felt her wet cunt enveloping him.

While he fucked her, she raked her nails across his back. It hurt like hell, but it just made him want to fuck her harder, like he was fighting her. She kept running her nails down his back and he knew she was drawing blood. It didn't deter him one bit.

"You like being hurt?" she said, gasping with his thrusts. "You love it, don't you?"

She plunged her nails into his back, pushing him aside and forcing him under her. She rode him as she scratched at his neck and slapped his face. She wasn't wrong. He'd never been more turned on in his life.

"You really love it, you fucking pig!" she hissed.

She wrapped her hands tight around his neck. Her hips pumped faster and faster. He knew he was going to cum soon. He tried to tell her, but her hands had shut off his vocal cords. She could obviously tell anyway.

"Cum, you fucking pig!"

He felt himself explode inside of her. The pain in his back, his chest, and neck all blended into the white-hot intensity of his orgasm.

When he tried to breathe a sigh of relief, he realized his air was still cut off. The look in her eyes said she had no intention of letting go. He started thrashing, pulling at her arms, and trying to squirm away. Even though he was bigger than her, the combination of alcohol, post-coital weakness, and the lack of air kept him from being able to push her off.

Her sadistic grin was the last thing he saw before everything went black.

SEVENTEEN

***CHRIS SITS IN A** pew in a church. He looks around. All the other pews are empty. He gets up. He tries to walk up the aisle to the exit. The exit seems to move away. He runs. He can't get any closer. He runs faster and faster. He still doesn't get anywhere. He runs until he collapses in exhaustion. He looks around again. He hasn't moved past the pew he got up from. He looks toward the tabernacle. A large wooden cross is hung up. Red light surrounds it. There is a door under it. Chris feels a deep sense of dread. He gets up and tries moving toward the tabernacle. He looks at the door and back at the exit. He does not want to go in that door. He knows he can't go anywhere else. He walks around the altar. He heads to the door. He grasps the doorknob. He turns it.*

EIGHTEEN

CHRIS OPENED HIS EYES. He realized he was looking up at an unfamiliar ceiling. He rubbed his eyes and yawned as the memories of last night came flooding back. His neck, back, and chest still ached.

"Baby, did you have to be that rough?" he said.

He turned, expecting to see Elaine next to him. Not only was she not there but he realized he was on a small bed not even big enough for two people. He sat up and looked around. The walls were off-white, and the floor was hardwood. His clothes were folded on the floor next to him beside his shoes. In front of him, there was a vault door. Still naked, he got up and tried to open the door. It wouldn't move. He tried forcing the handle, banging on the door screaming.

"Hey! Let me out! Goddammit! Open this fucking door!"

After a few minutes, he took another look around the room. He realized there was a simple wooden door on the other side of the vault. He ran to it and opened it. Inside was a bathroom that looked like the kind found in cheap but well-maintained motels. There were towels on a rack on the wall, miniature bottles of soap and shampoo on the sink, and a couple extra rolls of toilet paper on top of the toilet. Chris looked around. There were no other doors or windows and the only vent was about the size of his hand. He slammed the door.

He walked over to where his clothes were and started fishing in the pockets of his jeans. He found his keys and wallet, but his phone wasn't there. He beat his fists on the floor.

"God-fucking-dammit! I knew that bitch was crazy! I knew this town was fucked! Why did I come back here!"

He buried his face in his hands. He felt his head pounding and his stomach turning faster and faster. He shot back up and ran to the bathroom. He lifted the toilet lid and vomited. When he finished, he stood there bent over the toilet, breathing heavy and staring at his vomit without looking at it.

"Fuck!" he shouted as he hit the handle to flush.

He walked over to the sink and washed his face. After he dried off, he breathed deeply.

"Okay, okay. Whining won't change anything. I'm just going to clean up and figure out what the fuck to do."

He showered, brushed his teeth, shaved with the toiletries in the mirror cabinet, and got dressed. He went back to the bed and sat down.

What to do? he thought. *What the fuck to do?*

He looked around the room again. He got up, put his ear to the wall, and knocked on it. It sounded solid. He moved around the room, knocking around the wall.

There's got to be a weaker part I can brute force through.

He made his way around the room, standing on the bed to try the ceiling as well. He went into the bathroom and did the same, standing on the toilet to reach the ceiling.

Nothing. Goddammit!

He sat back on the bed. He stared at the wall. He replayed all his interactions with Elaine from when he met her on the beach to coming back to her apartment last night, then got distracted by the emptiness in his stomach.

Damn, I'm hungry. Unless she's planning to starve me to death, she's got to come and give me food at some point. Maybe I can rush her then.

He put his head on the pillow and stared up at the ceiling.

Chris tried to fall asleep a few times but found himself too wired. His mind kept flashing back to what happened the night before. He went back in the bathroom and splashed cold water on his face. When that didn't calm him down, he did push-ups and jumping jacks until he was tired. As he lay in bed, the memory of Elaine riding him with her hands tight around his neck kept running through his head. He muttered and stomped into the bathroom.

He jerked off, thinking about the way Elaine forced him under her, calling him a pig. He groaned and shot his load into the toilet. He grabbed some toilet paper to clean himself when he heard the vault door opening. He tossed the toilet paper in the bowl and looked back in the room. He saw the door beginning to open slightly. He was about to rush the door when he heard Elaine call to him.

"I have a gun," she said. "Don't try anything."

Chris started as he heard a gunshot go off and hit the outside of the door.

"Okay, okay!" he shouted. "What do you want?"

"First, strip yourself nude."

He did as she said, leaving his clothes where he'd found them when he'd woken up.

"Now what?"

Elaine opened the door farther and tossed a pair of handcuffs inside.

"Get on the bed and handcuff yourself to one of the bars on the headboard."

As he put the handcuff around his wrist he made sure not to actually secure it.

"Okay! I did it."

Elaine opened the door and came in. She was wearing a bathrobe and holding a Glock 17 in front of her, keeping it aimed at Chris. The first thing she did was check his handcuffs. When she realized it wasn't secure, she tightened it until he winced in pain.

"Naughty boy," she said, pressing the barrel of the gun against his forehead. "Now be good and listen. Put your other hand up."

She pulled another pair of handcuffs from her bathrobe pocket and cuffed his other hand to the bed, tightening it just as much as the other one.

"Ouch!"

"Well, if you just listen, then I won't have to hurt you."

She ran the barrel of the gun down his chest and toward his crotch. She pointed it at his half-hard cock and giggled.

"What's this?" she said.

She ran her finger around the head of his cock.

"It's wet. You were playing with yourself, weren't you?"

He didn't answer. She stuck the gun under his chin.

"I asked you a question."

"Yes! Yes, I was!"

"Bad boy. You don't play with yourself from now on. Understand?"

He nodded.

"Good, good."

She knelt and grabbed his balls, pulling them until he groaned and clenched his teeth in pain. His cock got fully hard. She took it in her mouth, running her tongue around the head and sucking on it. She sucked him off until he felt he was about to cum again, then she took her mouth off. His cock twitched, begging for release.

"Poor baby," she said in a patronizing voice. "You want to cum again?"

Chris shut his eyes and nodded.

Fuck! I do, and I hope that's the right answer, he thought.

He felt Elaine's fist smash into his face.

"Cum, you little pig!" she said.

She hit him again.

"You worthless little pervert!"

As she beat his face and insulted him, he felt his cock twitching more.

"You deserve this, you piece of shit!"

Finally, when she spit in his face and hit him again, he felt his warm cum spray all over his torso.

"There," she said. "Do you feel better, little piggy?"

The humiliation, pain in his face, and everything that had happened all caught up to him. He burst out crying.

"Let me go! Please! Please just let me go home!"

"Oh, poor baby."

She ran her fingers through her hair, cooing to him.

"I can't let you go. We've got too much planned for you."

"Who's we?"

"You'll find out soon enough, my cute little piggy."

She stuck the barrel back in his face. He went quiet.

"Now, I'm going to undo the cuffs. Move and I'll have to blow off your pretty little face."

He nodded. She took the cuffs off, keeping the gun pointed at his head. She stuck them in her robe pocket and backed out of the room. When she was out, she slowly closed the vault door. Before she slammed it shut, she tossed a brown paper bag into the room.

"There's your lunch, my sweet pig."

When the door was shut, he got off the bed. He rubbed his wrist, bruised from the tight cuffs around them. He went back into the bathroom and got in the shower. He turned the water on, making sure it was good and hot. After he washed the semen off his body, he sat down on the floor of the shower and cried some more.

NINETEEN

CHRIS WASN'T SURE HOW long he'd been in the room Elaine was keeping him prisoner in. There were no clocks and no windows. He guessed it about a week based on how often she'd brought his "lunch" and his "dinner." It was usually a simple sandwich, piece of fruit, and a can of soda water.

What he hated most was the pain and humiliation that came with his food.

Every time she came in, she would find new ways to sexually torture him at gunpoint. Once, she brought a bowl of chili and made him strip and eat it off the floor like a dog while she masturbated. Another time, she forced him into the bathroom and made him lie down on the floor of the tub and drink her piss. She sat on his face until he thought he was going to suffocate to death. She squeezed his balls until it felt like they were about to burst. She stuck pins in his nipples while giggling. She edged him for what felt like hours until he was begging. She cut the word "pig" into his chest with a knife. He felt lucky if all she did was ride him while choking him until he passed out.

Just as bad as the pain was the humiliation. When she tortured him, he was incredibly turned on. She rubbed that in every time. When she left him alone to eat, he felt incredibly dirty. He usually ended up crying in the shower.

Between that, it was nothing but boredom. He had nothing to do except pace the room, nap, exercise, or just stare at the wall. He'd tried asking her for a book, something to listen to music with, anything at all to make the time go by faster. She would just laugh, tell him he was in no position to ask for anything, or just ignore him altogether.

He wasn't sure how much more he could take. He was quickly losing hope he'd ever leave alive. Primavera knew where he was, and she had to have called the police by now, but how would they find him? He suspected the whole town was in on this, including the local police, so who would talk?

Whenever Elaine was in the throes of ecstasy riding his cock, she'd moan things like how she couldn't wait to see him bled out like a pig. He'd yell and demand to know what the hell she was talking about, but she would only hit him or stick the barrel of her gun in his mouth.

He knew they were planning to kill him, but he didn't know why. He thought it might be for religious reasons. The town seemed to hold that crazy priest in high regard. Maybe he had them practicing human sacrifice.

Whatever the reason, he knew he had to get out of there. He made up his mind. The next time Elaine came, he was going to rush her. He knew he'd probably get shot to death, but he didn't see any other way out. Besides, at this point he was beginning to believe it was a much better fate than what Elaine, both the town and the woman keeping him hostage, had planned for him.

He'd gathered his resolve the night before. It was still there when he woke up. He put on his clothes and shoes and sat in the front of the bed watching the door, waiting for her to open it slightly and bark orders at him.

Come on. Come on, you fucking cunt.

It felt like an eternity until he finally saw the door start to open. When it was open just enough he sprang up and ran to it. He threw his entire body weight against the door, forcing it farther open and knocking her back. He leaped at her, bracing himself for the bullet he knew was coming. It didn't come. As soon as he was on top of the figure on the floor, he realized it wasn't her.

"Karl?"

He lay beneath Chris with his arms up in surrender. His hands were shaking. He looked like he hadn't shaved or slept since he disappeared. Chris gaped at him and then grabbed him by his shirt collar.

"Where the fuck have you been!" he screamed. "What is . . ."

"Shush!" Karl said, gesturing his finger in front of his lips. "Be quiet!"

Chris heard a scuttling and a loud barking from the hallway. There was scraping and scratching, the barking growing louder and more frantic. It took him a moment to process. He couldn't believe that friendly Malamute from before was the thing sounding like a demon dog outside, scratching and biting and barking at the closed door. Then he remembered how Elaine turned and knew it wasn't all that strange of a fact.

"Shit!" Karl said. "That's what I was afraid of. He was asleep when I came in. That dog will rip us to shreds if he gets in here."

"What the hell is going on? You're in on this, aren't you? I'm going to feed you to that fucking dog and get out of here."

"No, no! Look, I didn't want this. I tried to make them stop, but they wouldn't listen."

"Who wouldn't listen?"

"All of them. I don't have time to explain. We have to get out."

Chris looked around. There was only one place to go besides back in the room behind the vault door.

"The window."

Chris jumped off Karl and ran to the window. He felt around it. There was no way to open it.

"Fuck!"

He put his hand on the wall and started kicking at the window. His foot kept bouncing off, doing no real damage.

"The fuck is this thing made of!"

He heard a banging on the door, followed by a yelp and more barking. He turned around. There was another bang and yelp. The door was starting to give. He didn't know how the dog was smart enough to throw itself against the door.

"Help with the window, Karl!"

"We don't have time! Here!"

Karl tossed a set of keys to Chris. He caught it.

"Take the truck. It's right outside," Karl said. "I'll distract the dog."

"What? No! We can—"

The door made a loud crack as the jamb started to give. Karl moved himself closer to it.

"I deserve this for how I've helped them with all those horrible things," he said, his voice cracking. "I'm so sorry. Agnes is sorry, too. She told me to tell you she still loves you."

"Where is—"

The door came crashing open. The Malamute sprinted into the room. It was definitely the same dog from the beach, but any friendliness was gone from his face. It lunged for Karl, knocking him to the ground and sinking his teeth into his throat.

Chris gaped in shock, hearing Karl gurgle and cough up blood as the dog tore into his neck. He looked at the keys in his hand and ran out of the room. As he got to the front door, he looked behind him. The dog was coming for him, his mouth red and a piece of muscle from Karl's neck hanging from his teeth. He ran through the front door and slammed it behind him. He headed down the stairs and out of the building.

As Karl said, the truck was parked next to the curb. He jumped in the cab. He tried a couple of the keys until one of them slid into the ignition. He turned the truck on and backed out of the parking spot. He took one last look at the building then put his foot down on the gas.

TWENTY

CHRIS DROVE THE TRUCK up the street. It took him a few minutes of running around Elaine's downtown until he got onto a street that led him out. A sign indicating the miles until Broken Bowl and some other towns he didn't take the time to read showed him he was going the right way.

The buildings on either side thinned out until there was nothing but woods. He kept driving until he came to a section of road that was torn up and blocked off by road closed signs. Beyond it, a bulldozer, trucks, cranes, and steamrollers were lined up as if forming a blockade. Even if he drove past the signs and over the torn section of road, they were lined up to the edge of the woods where the trees were too thick to take the truck through.

He parked on the side of the road and made his way past the signs.

Fuck it. If I have to walk all the way back, I will, he thought.

As he approached the construction vehicles, someone came out from behind one of the trucks. He was a tall man with a thick red beard, a hard hat, and a bright yellow vest.

"Hey!" the road worker yelled. "Didn't you see the signs?"

"I need to get out of town."

"Find some other way. Road's closed."

"Where's the nearest road out?"

"Beats me."

"Look, I need to get out."

"Not my problem. Get out of here."

"Look, just let me . . ."

"Get out of here before I get in that bulldozer and run your ass over!"

The sudden bellowing startled Chris. He ran back across the torn-up road, nearly falling on his face, and hopped back into the truck. He turned around. As he drove back the way he came, he checked the rear-view mirror. The road worker was standing with his arms crossed and a hateful look on his face.

Chris drove straight to the train station. He parked in the gravel lot and ran to the door. As he feared, it was locked. He kicked the door repeatedly.

"Son of a fucking bitch!"

As he stomped back to the truck, he grabbed a handful of gravel from the lot and threw it at the windows. It bounced off without causing any damage. He got in the truck and continued farther up the road, heading toward the Porcupine Mountains.

There has to be another road out.

As he drove, he kept looking in the rear-view mirror and to either side. There was occasionally a home or a gravel road, but it was mostly woods. He was forced to stop when he came to a dead-end sign. Nothing was behind it but woods and beyond that the mountains.

He slammed his fist against the wheel and turned the truck around. He slowed down when he started approaching Karl's house.

Should I grab my stuff? No, fuck it, they'll be looking for me there. I need to get out.

He felt his stomach tighten as he headed back downtown. There was still nobody out and about.

Thank Christ. If I see anybody, especially that Elaine bitch, I'm running them over. I don't give a fuck.

He took another road out of downtown. It led him down a row of houses. Most of them were one story and white with the occasional brown or white two-story. He drove until he came to a sudden dead end.

However, it didn't look like a dead end. It seemed to continue on normally, but something wasn't right. He felt like it was something from a Wile E. Coyote cartoon where he'd painted a landscape on a wall for the Roadrunner to crash into. Like the Roadrunner, he felt he could keep going into it, but it wouldn't take him to a safe place. He had the intense feeling he'd end up some place far worse than even this town if he went down that road.

As he sat there trying to comprehend what he was seeing, he caught a movement out of the corner of his eye. He looked and saw Pastor Toivo and his wife standing on the lawn of the house next to him. The pastor was pointing a shotgun at him. He began to approach the car, making a gesture to roll down the window.

Chris threw the car in reverse and slammed on the gas. He looked over his shoulder, reversing the vehicle, the sound of the shotgun cracking around him. A gray tabby cat ran into the road. He didn't have time to swerve to avoid it. He felt the bump as the tire went over the cat. The cat's screaming was drowned out by another shotgun blast. He turned and saw the cat's body as he kept the truck in reverse. Its stomach had burst on the road and its blood and intestines spilled out on the pavement. Farther up the road, the pastor was running toward him and aiming the shotgun. He raised it and took another shot that missed. He stopped as Chris got farther away, yelling something he couldn't hear.

Chris got the truck turned around before he hit downtown. He looked around frantically as he went up the street.

Only one thing left to do. There's no one here that can help me. I've got to get back to the train station. I need to get on that track and follow it back to Broken Bowl. I'll just pray there's no trains coming.

He heard a police siren start up behind him. In the rear view, the lights on the police car were flashing. It trailed him closely behind. He sped up.

The police car trailed him until he left downtown and hit the road to the train station. He heard a gunshot. He looked in the mirror. It was the police officer, Matt, in the car. He was leaning out the window and firing. Chris tried swerving to avoid the shots. There was a loud burst as a bullet hit the rear right tire.

He gripped the wheel, calmly turning it to keep the truck on the road.

Don't crash. Don't crash. You're fucked if you crash.

He stabilized the truck, rim screeching as it scraped the curb.

The police car drew closer in the rear-view mirror. Pushing the gas farther down wasn't putting much distance between them.

He realized he was getting close to Karl's house. He jerked the wheel, barreling toward the woods.

I hope this works.

He slammed on the brakes, stopping just before the truck crashed head first into a tree. He turned the truck off and pulled the keys out of the ignition. As he hopped out of the truck, the police car was slowed to a stop.

He turned to the woods and ran into them as fast as he could.

TWENTY-ONE

OH, THANK GOD, Chris thought as he came upon Karl's home.

He hadn't been sure he was running the right way. He opened the door, thankful he didn't have to waste time unlocking it, shut it behind him, and locked it. He headed straight for the locked door he thought led to Karl's room.

There's got to be a gun or something in there.

He tried the different keys on the ring until one of them slid in and turned. He ran into the room. It didn't look much different from the guest bedroom he'd been staying in upstairs, except it was bigger. He ran to the closet. He pulled the various hanging shirts aside. No gun.

He pulled the three boxes on the floor of the closet out. He pulled one open. It was full of papers. All of them were typewritten. A quick glance at it showed they were typed in Finnish. The second was filled with women's clothes. The third had nothing but paperback books. He kicked one of the boxes.

He ran over to the dresser. He pulled the clothes out, throwing them all over the floor.

Where's a fucking gun?

When he opened the bottom drawer, it was empty except for a green book that said "Photos" on the cover. He picked it up and opened it. A piece of paper fell out. He picked it up and read it

.

If you find this, please burn it. Don't look at it. Just burn it.
—KJ

He opened the book. The first Polaroid photo he saw was of a naked prepubescent girl. A hand coming from out of frame was forcing her legs apart. Her face was contorted in fear, tears running down her face. Looking closely, he could tell the little girl in the photo was Agnes. He threw the book aside.

"Fuck!"

He heard a banging at the front door. He ran out of the room. He saw the outline of Matt in the door's window. It sounded like he was kicking at it. He could see the jamb was going to give.

He ran into the kitchen and started opening the drawers. He grabbed the biggest knife he could find and ran out the door. He slammed it behind him as he heard the front door break down. He ran down the path to the beach, glancing behind him to make sure his pursuer wasn't there.

When he emerged at the beach, he stood and listened to the waves of Lake Superior. He closed his eyes and thought about where to go next. He remembered the rowboat at the house where Matt shot the old lady.

Getting away by water is a long shot, even if the boat's still there, but where the hell else do I go?

Gripping the knife, he ran up the beach. As he kicked up sand, he heard a frantic barking. It was getting closer and closer. He looked toward the woods. Elaine's Malamute came running out, its mouth still red with blood.

He tried running but the dog easily caught up, running in front of him and leaping for his throat. He put his arm up. The dog sank his teeth into his arm and knocked him down. Chris yelled as he felt the intense pain of the bite. He looked at the dog's face. His eyes were full of a desire to kill and taste more blood. The dog growled and pulled at his arm.

He tightened his fist around the knife's handle and plunged it into the dog's side. The dog yelped but kept his grip on Chris's arm. He closed his eyes and stabbed the dog again and again. Even after it stopped yelping, Chris kept stabbing until the dog's jaw went slack. He threw the dog's body off him. He sat up and looked at the dog's carcass, the wounds in his side spilling blood into the sand.

"Aww, how could you do that to Abe?" a woman's voice said.

He whipped his head around to the source. Elaine walked

toward him, her gun pointed at him. He froze.

"Just come back," Elaine said. "I could kill you right here, but I'll give you another chance. You'll get to be my little pig for a while longer. I know how much you love that. Then I'll make sure when they kill you, it's mostly painless. I know the smell of your blood will please God very much, so it would be a shame to lose you now."

As she got close to him, he grabbed a handful of sand and threw it in her face. She shrieked as the sand hit her eyes. She fired the gun but missed and hit the dog's body. It jerked as the bullet went into it.

Chris sprang up with the knife in front of him and plunged it into her stomach. She fell back, dropping her gun. As she lay in the sand coughing up blood, he grabbed the gun and stood over her. He pointed it at her head. She gasped for air.

"Chrissy," she said, "please don't."

He hesitated for a moment before he pulled the trigger. The bullet entered her forehead. Her blood and brains splashed into the sand underneath her head. The glassy, empty eyes on the body that used to be Elaine stared up at him. Her mouth hung open. Blood dribbled down her chin.

His hands trembled. Amy used to tease him by calling him Chrissy when they were both very young. She told him Mom had wanted another girl and that she dressed him in girl's clothes when he was too young to remember. She'd bring it up whenever she wanted to pick on him. Once, when she was being especially vindictive, she brought it up in front of a couple of his friends while they were over. He never heard the end of it at school. Even his friends joined in on humiliating him by calling him Chrissy and asking where his skirt was. He never forgave her for that.

There was no way Elaine would have been able to know that. He wondered if she really was his sister. It wasn't possible, though. No matter how much she looked like her. Even as long as it had been since he'd talked to her, he knew. Elaine acted nothing like her. Their parents still sent Amy cards and gifts for her birthday and Christmas that he'd often chip in for and sign. They always went to California, not Michigan.

He turned away from the dead woman. He ran back up the beach, the gun and the knife in his hands. He was running on autopilot. He barely grasped where he was until he finally got to the rowboat.

He took a quick look around. When he didn't see anyone, he tossed the gun and knife into the boat. The oars were inside of the boat. He pushed it out as far as he could, feeling the water soak into his shoes and the legs of his jeans. He climbed inside and grabbed the oars. He rowed as fast as he could away from the shore, keeping his eye toward it as he pumped his arms. The pain of the dog bite was drowned out by the adrenaline rushing through him.

When he was far away from the shore, he pulled the oars back into the boat and set them to his sides. He slid on to the floor of the boat. Exhaustion was catching up to him. He started to quietly cry. He covered his face with his hands and listened to the sounds of the lake until he calmed down. He put his arms to his side and fell asleep.

TWENTY-TWO

CHRIS SEES WHITE. *He sees black. He sees blue. He sees the vague shapes of faces in the colors. He hears the sounds of Lake Superior. Underneath, he hears barks, screams, and gun shots. The sounds of the lake get louder and drowns them out. A cool breeze sweeps across his body. It eases the pain in his arm.*

TWENTY-THREE

CHRIS JOLTED AWAKE. He looked around, realizing he was still in the rowboat. He grinned and started laughing.

"I got away! I got the fuck away! Fuck all of you!"

He breathed deep and took another look around. He couldn't see the shore anywhere around.

Where do I go now?

He looked at the dog bite on his arm. It wasn't bleeding anymore but it still hurt. He touched it and winced.

Goddammit! I hope that doesn't get infected.

He sighed and grabbed the oars, trying to ignore the sharp pain in his arm.

Guess I just need to keep rowing. Just like the end of that shitty-ass Great Gatsby *book.*

TWENTY-FOUR

HE WASN'T SURE HOW long he'd been rowing. It felt like days, but the sun didn't go down once. At least, it didn't seem like it. Thick clouds had rolled in and now everything seemed to be in a perpetual early morning or late afternoon light. He wondered if he just missed night when he lay down to sleep, though he couldn't keep track of it. He just kept rowing and sleeping when he was tired enough. At some point, the sounds of the waves stopped. He couldn't hear anything coming from the lake but the oars moving through the water. However, whenever he lay down to sleep, he swore he heard something else. At times it sounded like a heart beat, other times a refrigerator humming, and often it was a noise he couldn't describe. He didn't find them unpleasant. They calmed him and sang him to sleep the same way the waves had.

The dog bite on his arm didn't seem to be getting any better, but it wasn't getting any worse either. He got hungry and tried to use the knife to get fish from the lake, but he couldn't catch anything. He scooped up handfuls of the water to avoid dehydration, thankful the lake was freshwater.

As he kept going, it was getting colder and colder. Constantly rowing was helping to keep him warm, but he still wished he had a coat. He now had to huddle in a ball when he went to sleep, and he woke up shivering.

He thought he saw a sheet of ice go floating by the boat, but he thought he had to be hallucinating. There was no way it could be that cold, even if he was somehow getting close to Canada. Then he started seeing more and more. It was like wherever the lake was taking him, it had somehow pushed him past all of Canada and into the Arctic Circle. He thought about turning around, but he'd gotten so disoriented he wasn't sure which way he'd come to get here.

It was freezing cold and now he was having to row to avoid the increasing thick masses of ice floating around him. He avoided going to sleep, afraid he wouldn't wake up. Soon, the ice was unavoidable. The boat rocked as he continued running into the chunks of ice. He prayed the boat would hold.

Finally, the boat ran aground on a large mass of ice and snow. With nowhere else to go, he climbed out and set off across the arctic landscape. He trudged along, his arms wrapped around himself. He rubbed his arms to keep warm as he kept walking. The snow seemed to get deeper and deeper.

After a while, he saw a figure in the distance. As he got closer, it seemed like it was a person. He ran toward them, having to raise his legs higher and higher to move through the snow. When he got close enough, he finally recognized the person.

"Agnes!"

She stood wearing a thick fur coat, buried up to her waist in the snow. She held out her arm and waved him to her. He sprinted toward her. When he got to her, he took a moment to look closely at her. She didn't seem to be a hallucination. She smiled at him.

He started bawling and wrapped his arms around her. She held him close and whispered to him.

"It's okay," she said.

Her voice was like a mix of high winds and the waves of Lake Superior whispering to him.

"I'm so sorry," she said. "I didn't want this to happen. I told them to leave you alone."

"I'm so sorry, too," he said through his tears. "I thought you just up and left. I met this girl you know named Elaine and . . ."

"Shh. Shh. I know. It's okay. You're here now. I'll keep you warm and safe."

She opened the fur coat and wrapped it around him. The warmth and the sweet smell of her skin enveloped him. Around them, the wind started picking up. Snow started falling hard and fast. It was impossible to see beyond a few feet. He didn't care. He couldn't see or feel any of it. The snow could have buried them both completely right there and it wouldn't have bothered him at all.

EPILOGUE

From the Monk City Tribune

TWO MONK CITY RESIDENTS REPORTED MISSING

Monk City residents Chris Vogel, 31, and Agnes Jespersen, 28, have been reported missing to police. Vogel is the owner of Snoring Records, a two-time nominee for the best record store in the city by *The Monk Metro*. Jespersen, according to friends and family, was his girlfriend and an employee at Axis Insurance. The two were reported missing by Primavera Cortez, an employee at Snoring Records.

According to Cortez, he had left her in charge of the store while he went to Elaine, Michigan. Jespersen had gone up for the funeral of her recently deceased mother and Chris followed her after he had made his arrangements with the store.

"He apparently couldn't find her when he got up there," Cortez said. "Then he started contacting me, telling me he was afraid and that he thought he was in danger. He told me to go to the police if I didn't hear back from him after a while."

Monk City Police stated they have contacted both the police department of Elaine and the

Broken Bowl County Sheriff's Office. The Broken Bowl County Sheriff was able to locate Vogel's car outside of an abandoned shack on the edge of the town of Broken Bowl but found nothing else indicating where he may have gone. The Elaine police have stated they have been unable to find any evidence or witnesses stating that Vogel had come to the town. At this time, the Broken Bowl County Sheriff suspects there may be a connection with the recent disappearance of two teenagers from Ironhorse, Michigan who were last seen by a truck driver who gave them a ride and dropped them off in Broken Bowl.

Despite the report by Cortez claiming Agnes had called Elaine her hometown and was going for her mother's funeral, the Elaine Police Department claims they have no records of anyone with the surname Jespersen either residing in the town or recently passing away.

Vogel's parents, Mitchell and Peggy, said they are now offering a $1,000 reward for any information leading to their son's whereabouts.

"We're worried sick," Peggy Vogel said. "When Pri (Cortez) told us what happened, we knew something was wrong. He cared so deeply for Agnes and for his record store. Both were his whole world. He'd never just up and disappear like this. We called his sister, Amy, in San Francisco and she hasn't heard from him either. Not that those two ever talked much since she moved out."

None of Agnes Jespersen's relatives could be reached for comment.

Thank you, Kitten, for all your love and support.
Thank you to my family for encouraging me.
Thank you to Andersen Prunty and C.V. Hunt for believing in this book.

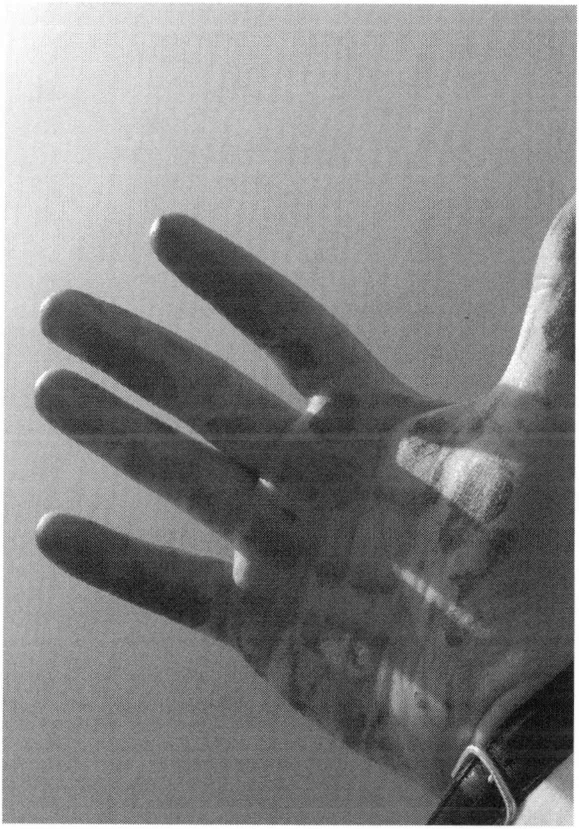

Ben Arzate lives in Des Moines, Iowa. He is a regular contributor to Cultured Vultures and Silent Motorist Media. His poetry and prose has appeared in several places in print and online. Find him online at http://dripdropdripdropdripdrop.blogspot.com

Other **Atlatl Press** Books

Bird Castles by Justin Grimbol
Fuck Happiness by Kirk Jones
Impossible Driveways by Justin Grimbol
Giraffe Carcass by J. Peter W.
Shining the Light by A.S. Coomer
Failure As a Way of Life by Andersen Prunty
Hold for Release Until the End of the World
by C.V. Hunt
Die Empty by Kirk Jones
Mud Season by Justin Grimbol
Death Metal Epic (Book Two: Goat Song Sacrifice)
by Dean Swinford
Come Home, We Love You Still by Justin Grimbol
We Did Everything Wrong by C.V. Hunt
Squirm With Me by Andersen Prunty
Hard Bodies by Justin Grimbol
Arafat Mountain by Mike Kleine
Drinking Until Morning by Justin Grimbol
Thanks For Ruining My Life by C.V. Hunt
Death Metal Epic (Book One: The Inverted Katabasis)
by Dean Swinford
Fill the Grand Canyon and Live Forever by Andersen Prunty
Mastodon Farm by Mike Kleine
Fuckness by Andersen Prunty
Losing the Light by Brian Cartwright
They Had Goat Heads by D. Harlan Wilson
The Beard by Andersen Prunty

Thank you for helping to support Atlatl Press.

Made in the USA
Monee, IL
25 May 2020

31641158R00065